Megan,

My Paper Heart

Follow your heart

Magan Vernon

Copyright © 2012 by Magan Vernon
Http://www.maganvernon.com

This book is a work of fiction. Names, characters, places, and incidents are either products of the author's imagination or used fictitiously. Any resemblance to actual events, locales, or persons, living or dead, is entirely coincidental. All rights reserved. No part of this publication can be reproduced or transmitted in any form by or any means, electronic or mechanical, without permission in writing from the author.

Print Edition: March 2014

First edition edited by Looking Glass editing

Cover by Elizabeth Sharp at Sharp Cover Designs

FOR RACHEL

You saw this book as something special and made me never give up

ACKNOWLEDGMENTS

This book was a true labor of love. It has been everything from upper YA to women's fiction and finally came back to the story it is today. I never thought this book would actually end up on someone's Ereader or the Amazon homepage, so to the person reading this I thank you.

Three years later and I can't forget the people that first read this book: Kelly Viel, Jennifer Dallman, Lynsey Newton, Leta Gail Doerr, Laurie Larsen, Nicole Settle, Steph Bowe, and Kelsey Ketch. Thank you for seeing the potential in this book.

To Rachel Tiderman, there were years that we were on the outs and then I brought this book to you. You never let me give up on these characters and you are the reason this book is being published.

To my wonderful husband, Tim, you sat by and watched me fail insurance tests because I was too busy working on this book and still supported me. Without you, none of this would be possible.

Olivia, my darling little girl, Libby's name was originally Olivia Grace Gentry and then I had an Olivia of my own and didn't want to share the spotlight.

To Marcie at Looking Glass Editing, thank you for slicing commas when they needed and keeping the ones I would not give up.

To the Indelibles, we've all had our ups and downs in this crazy world of publishing and I'm so happy that I have all of you to keep my head above water.

Finally, to the beautiful landscape of Louisiana that inspired this story. If I could I would spend every day in Café Du Monde and living in the beauty of the French Quarter.

CHAPTER 1

Mom held the piece of paper in her hands. It was as if she was holding my heart. Thin and frail. My paper heart to be torn to shreds.

"Elizabeth Libby Gentry's grade's have not been able to meet the required 2.0 grade point average for two semesters; therefore she will **not** be welcomed back to Illinois State University for the fall semester," my mom read out loud, emphasizing not as if it was the dirtiest word she had ever heard.

"Mom, it's not like I tried to fail out." I held my hands out, as if my excuse was some kind of gift that I had wrapped up and presented to her.

My parents sat across the dining room table from me — Mom, with the letter in her hand and my dad with his fingers wrapped around a glass of bourbon. I had been waiting for this conversation ever since the letter came in the mail. I had mentally prepared myself for the worst.

Over the past few days I had weighed my options.

I could go to community college (I had dealt with drunken frat guys for a whole year, so I was pretty sure that I could deal with a few creepy old men in class). Or maybe working in my dad's office (screaming kids with cavities were not exactly the way that I wanted to spend my day. I had enough of that in my sorority). The different scenarios played in my head over and over again. Clearly my parents had been doing the same thing since they had come up with an idea as well.

My dad swirled his drink in his hands, not taking his eyes off while he sighed. His fingers traced the rim of the crystal glass. His body may have been facing toward me, but his eyes told me that he wanted to be nowhere near me. He did everything he could to avoid looking at me. It was as if I was some sort of criminal instead of his own daughter.

"Libby, your father and I have been discussing your predicament." My mother folded her hands on the table. "We have decided that you should go work for your Great Aunt Dee."

I stopped twirling my long blonde waves and stared at my mother. Our brown eyes met before she looked back at my father and patted his knee. My mother could pretend that she was the big hot shot lawyer all she wanted, but in the Gentry house my father was always the patriarch. She always looked to him for approval.

I wished I had her courage though. Even as she looked at my dad, brushing her golden hair out of her eyes, she still carried herself like she was the most important woman in the world. She would never let a guy tell her that she had to drop a few pounds before she could be his date to formal, or stop going to class because she didn't know what the hell an acute angle was and was too afraid to ask.

"We both think this would be the best thing for you. I'll drive you down to the bus station tomorrow morning and then you'll leave for Louisiana," she said it as if it were just something simple.

"LOUISIANA? GREAT AUNT DEE?" I screeched. "Can we just back this up here? I mean, don't I get a say in this?"

Dad sighed again and stood up, the lines in his forehead crinkling as he spoke. "Libby. You messed up. There's nothing else I can really say about that. Aunt Dee agreed that you could stay with her for a while and work at her shop. Think about it Libby, do you really think you're going to find a job here? With your experience you may be able to get a job flipping burgers."

I opened my mouth to say something, but I knew he was right. It's wasn't like I ever had a job before and I definitely wasn't the fast food working type. A hairnet really wasn't my style.

"Maybe this will give you some time to think, and you can enroll somewhere else in the fall." Then dad gave me his signature, this conversation is over, don't say another word or I'm going to lose my cool, look and I knew there was no getting out of it.

Dad nodded to my mother and headed into the den; probably to pour himself another drink and pass out in front of the Cubs game. Mom reached across the table for my hand, like it would actually give me some comfort.

"I'm going for a run." I mumbled, defeated as I

sprang from the table. I didn't even bother to look back as I slipped into my shoes and ran out the front door, down the cobblestone driveway.

Running was a sure fire way to get rid of my problems. I literally felt like I was running nowhere, with nowhere to go and no one to be waiting for me. I ran every morning with my pledge class to make sure that I made weekly weigh-ins. I ran as quickly as I could through my notes before a test hoping that I would actually be able to remember something on a test. And on that last night of finals I just happened to run into my boyfriend going down on my roommate.

Maybe running wasn't such a bad thing after all. If I ran to Louisiana then maybe I could run away from everything back home and just forget about Chicago. Forget that I had no place else to go.

There was nothing that I could say to my parents that would change their minds. I figured that they had already formed their opinion, that I had turned into some drunk, partying co-ed, anyway. I wondered if they even cared to know the real Libby. I wondered if anyone actually ever would.

CHAPTER 2

"Couldn't I have at least flown to Louisiana? I mean it could have been like eleven hours less time, and I could have started working right away!" I scoffed and slung my purse over my shoulder. Mom rolled her eyes and pulled my suitcase out of the trunk of her car.

"The airport is at least an hour from Aunt Dee's, and we wouldn't want to inconvenience her even more. She's doing us a big enough favor by taking you in. The least we can do is give her a shorter drive by having her pick you up at the bus station in town."

"I could drive my own car. I mean, it's just going to be sitting in the driveway for who knows how long." My black flip flops flapped on the pavement as we started toward the Greyhound station.

My mom stopped abruptly and sighed. "Call us when you get there." She handed me the tickets and started walking toward her car.

I turned on my heels. "That's it? No hug? No I'll miss you?" I started briskly walking after her, the waistband of my designer sweatpants falling down on my hips. I reached down and slowly pulled them up while I stood staring at my mom.

"Look, Libby." She turned toward me and put her hands on my shoulders. "Your father and I love you,

you know that, but you also know how upset we are with you right now. I think you have some growing up to do."

I couldn't meet my mom's eyes. It was that same look of disappointment she wore all week. Instead I stared at the other people that were boarding the bus: mothers sending off their kids and wiping the hair out of their eyes, friends holding each other like it would be the last time that they would ever see the other, and I definitely couldn't ignore the boyfriends and girlfriends kissing goodbye. My ex, Beau, never kissed me like that. There was one couple in which the boy would give the girl one long kiss with a short peck after, like he was sealing it. The couple looked my way and I quickly turned, hoping that they hadn't noticed me staring at them. I focused back on my mom, trying to grasp on to that last bit of comfort of home.

"Someday you will learn that life is not all about partying and texting, and by then, hopefully, we'll be ready to have you come home."

She kissed my forehead, and I watched her walk back toward her car. I knew then it would be the last time I would smell her perfume or hear her laugh for a long time. I ran my fingers through my ponytail, grabbed my suitcase, and climbed into the bus. Fourteen hours of pure pleasure were surely ahead of me.

∞

I was the last one on the bus. Everyone had already picked their seat near someone they knew, or just someone to talk to on the long ride ahead. Everyone tried to make themselves as comfortable as they could in the bright pink and green bus seats. They looked like they were something straight out of the eighties and probably were just about as comfortable as the furniture that you'd find in the waiting areas of hospitals.

I finally reached the back of the bus to an open seat in the back and near the window. I saw the girl with the longing boyfriend out of the corner of my eye. He was gone, but she was staring at her phone and smiling as she typed away. She knew exactly where she was going and didn't have to run.

I unlocked my phone and looked down at the blinking screen.

One new text message.

I unlocked my phone and smiled as I saw the message.

New Message from Kappa Kristi:

You better not run away with some southern boy and not come to my wedding!

I replied back.

Dun worry. Even the Louisiana heat can't keep me away from your wedding...and I really doubt I will find a boy in Podunk.

I put my phone back into my bag and made myself comfortable in the seat. Like hell I would miss my sorority sister's wedding. One of the compromises I made with my parents before I left was that they had to get me a plane ticket to go home for Kristi's wedding in August. I was hoping by then that they would be ready for me to come home and maybe by that time I would be ready as well.

CHAPTER 3

The bus pulled into the Wal-Mart parking lot, which doubled as a station, at about four in the morning. I was tired from trying to sleep and failing miserably. I couldn't have been happier to finally get off the stupid bus. I wanted nothing more than to crawl into my bed, but I knew I wouldn't be doing that again for a while.

The last time that I saw Aunt Dee was at my grandma's funeral. All I knew about her was that she was my dad's mother's sister and that she owned tourist shop in some tiny town in Louisiana. Needless to say, I had no idea who to look for in the dimly lit parking lot.

"Elizabeth? Jesus help me, is that you?" A fiery haired lady walked toward me, squinting behind a pair of overly thick glasses. I scrutinized her dye job, which I was sure had to come from a drugstore bottle. At my five foot ten height I towered over this woman. She seemed a little confused as to whether I was the right person, or maybe her French braid was just a little too tight.

"Libby, call me Libby." I twirled a fallen curl between my fingers. "And you must be Aunt Dee?"

"Oh honey!" Aunt Dee wrapped her bare arms

around me as she embraced me in a hug. She was so short her head was practically buried in my chest. It was hot, with the kind of humidity that just chokes you as soon as you step outside. You could definitely smell the heat on Aunt Dee, sweat and swamp mist from what I gathered. It took all the energy I had left not to gag as I gently hugged her back.

She let go of me and looked me up and down. "You are just as pretty as a picture! You are going to be chasing these Elsbury boys off with a stick, which I'm sure is what you were doing at college..."She trailed off as she looked at my luggage. "I guess that is why you're here..." She looked back up at me. "Well enough about that, you must be exhausted. Let's get you home, I have your room all ready!" I grabbed my suitcase and followed Aunt Dee as her awful dirt brown clogs clicked on the pavement.

"Brittany is just so excited to have you. I mean it's been a while since we've had anyone in the house besides her and me." Aunt Dee searched through her hideous fake leather purse as we walked down the parking lot.

"Who is Brittany?" I cocked my head to the side as we reached Aunt Dee's car, an old, green Grand Am. It was obvious that I wasn't going to be riding in style. The car's frame creaked as I leaned against it. I wouldn't have been surprised if it just fell over, leaving only a cloud of rust and green paint behind.

Aunt Dee pushed her glasses up with her index finger and looked up at me. Her beady little brown eyes seemed to still carry a bit of a spark in them even if the rest of her face was so wrinkled; it almost looked like a lightly tanned prune.

"Oh, well I guess you wouldn't know Brittany." Aunt Dee unlocked the door and slid into the stained, gray seat. I tossed my suitcase into the back and climbed in.

She started the car. "Brittany is my granddaughter."

"Why doesn't she live with her mom then?" I looked down at my chipped nail polish, as she pulled out of the parking lot. I wondered if there was any place that I could get a manicure in this small town.

"Well, it's not something we like to bring up, but my daughter, Joni decided to follow her own path. She was the prettiest girl in the whole parish and a real nice girl." Her voice got dreamy as she reminisced, but then her tone changed to have more of a bitter taste, as if she were forcing herself to purge the words. "But that was years ago. After she graduated high school she got pregnant with Brittany. I really thought a baby would change her and really make us bond." You could almost see the struggle in Aunt Dee's voice as she spoke; it was like her tongue was literally fighting to get the words out. "But, sadly, it just made things worse. After Brittany was born, it was like she wanted nothing to do with that baby unless she could be sold for crack." Aunt Dee said crack with the same tone that my mom had said not when she read my letter from the school.

"Joni smoked them out of house and home, so about seven years ago, when Brittany was eight, I adopted her. That was right before Joni lost her life to that drug." She spilled it all out like she told the story every day.

I gulped. I hadn't been expecting her to divulge so

much, especially because we barely knew each other. But I suppose some people are just more trusting with their family members.

We zipped down the road. There were hardly any streetlights, so I couldn't see much of the town. From what I could make out in the darkness, there wasn't much to it. Before I knew it, we were pulling in to a long gravel driveway and into a weeping willow lined yard. Her house, which was about the size of my parents' garage, was definitely not what I expected someone who owned a business to have. Aunt Dee pulled into the carport on the side of the house and killed the engine.

"My late husband built this house for us over thirty years ago. It was his wedding present to me." A distant smiled spread across her face as she spoke.

I followed her down the cobblestone path and up to the small brick house. A big sign hung on front of the door.

And the rain descended, and the floods came, and the winds blew, and beat upon that house; and it fell not: for it was founded upon a rock.

It was scrolled across the big wooden sign, and I cocked my head trying to make out the meaning of it. Aunt Dee saw me looking at the sign and grabbed my hand. It was one of actual comfort that I hadn't felt from years for my own mother. Even when my mom tried to reach for me it was always like a chore, something that she struggled with since feelings weren't her strong suit. It was always that cold empathy that she commanded in the court room, not the warmth that Aunt Dee radiated from her. It made me realize how much I had longed for this sense of comfort for so long.

"The last hurricane took a lot from this town; St. Bernard Parish was probably hit the hardest next to New Orleans, but our house did not falter. We had some damage to the property, but this house stayed strong. With your Uncle Walter's bricklaying and my strength in God our house stayed intact. We were one of the lucky ones though, so many weren't so lucky." She patted my hand and unlocked the big, white door.

I followed her into the living room that was dimly lit by a small plastic lamp sitting on an end table.

"Brittany is sleeping, and I'm sure you're tired, so I'll show you to your bedroom and give you the tour in the morning," Aunt Dee whispered, her shoes clomping on the old wood floor.

I couldn't imagine there would be much to see. I had already seen the plaid furniture that cluttered the living room, and it looked like that opened up to the outdated yellow kitchen. I guessed bedrooms and bathrooms were all that we had left. I followed Aunt Dee down the short, narrow hallway, careful not to make too much noise.

"That's the bathroom," Aunt Dee whispered as she pointed at a closed door.

"There's only one bathroom?" I tried not to be too loud. Aunt Dee nodded, not losing her stride as she opened the door almost directly to the right of the bathroom. How could I live with one bathroom? I had a hard enough time in the dorms, sharing a bathroom with all the girls on my floor. Sharing a bathroom with two other women was not on my list of high priorities.

"And this is your room." Aunt Dee flipped on the lights. As my eyes adjusted, I wasn't pleased with what I saw. The room was barely bigger than my closet back home, and it looked stuffed with the twin bed, white wicker night stand, and a huge desk along one of the walls that was piled with what appeared to be craft supplies.

"Sorry, this has been my scrapbooking room for the past ten years, but I'm sure you can share with my supplies." She smiled as she patted me on the back. "This is Brittany's old bedding, but we can go to Wal-Mart later and see what we can find you for a comforter." I smiled weakly. I was so tired that I didn't have the energy to protest sleeping on the hideous bubblegum pink bedding.

Aunt Dee left me in the tiny room alone with my thoughts. I was lucky that I was so tired that there wasn't much time to think. I didn't even feel like exfoliating, washing my face, or even putting on my pajama pants. I turned off the lamp and collapsed into the cheap polyester comforter.

There was a window directly over the bed. Sheer, white curtains could barely keep out the moonlight that streamed in. There were more stars out than I could ever remember seeing anywhere. When I was younger I used to wish on stars all the time. Living near a big city, I couldn't see as many as there were here. My eyes slowly started to flutter and close as the grasshoppers chirped outside my window, and my last thoughts were of the stars, hoping that wishing on stars wasn't just a fairy tale, and maybe if I wished hard enough I could be back home.

CHAPTER 4

I could have slept all day long, but I awoke to the bright sunlight streaming in from the tiny window. I would have really been more upset if my nose didn't perk up to the smell of something amazing coming from the kitchen. The last time I had a home cooked meal was when I visited one of my sorority sisters over Christmas break. My mom didn't cook, and my dad definitely didn't get any of those southern cooking genes. I wiped my eyes and slid my feet out of the fluffy pink marshmallow cavern I had made for myself in the tiny bed. I squinted as I peered over at the pink alarm clock on the night stand. I was too tired to open my eyes all the way, but the sunlight was too harsh to keep them closed.

"Eight A.M.?" I sighed and stood up. If I was awake anyway, I might as well start off the rest of the first day of my new life in the south.

"Oh, it sounds like Libby is up!" I heard Aunt Dee yell over the sizzling sound of bacon.

I shuffled along the floor barely awake as the top of my sweatpants hung off of my hips. I made a point of double knotting the drawstring so they wouldn't fall. I wasn't sure how keen Aunt Dee would be to see my stomach, or anything else that could be seen for that matter.

It was hot out already, and even with Aunt Dee's fans blowing and the window air conditioning unit going, the cooking was just making it hotter. The house looked even more outdated in the daylight. The walls looked like they could use a few coats of paint and all the light fixtures looked like they were straight out of a museum. I wondered how Aunt Dee didn't notice all the work that needed to be done to the house, or if she even cared.

I rubbed my eyes to look and see where Brittany was. I thought since she was fifteen, she would be close enough to my age, maybe she could at least steer me in the direction of the closest mall. All I saw when I opened my eyes was what looked like a chubby, pasty boy with freckles and a bad black bowl cut.

"Where's Brittany?" I mumbled as I flopped down in the yellow plastic kitchen chair.

"I AM Brittany." An annoyed voice came from the other person at the table. Maybe I was wrong about it being a boy at the table, or that she would be able to point me in the direction of the mall. The girl was a hot mess!

She was chubby and short, probably around five feet tall. That would have been forgivable if she at least had some sense of style. Her black coarse hair was just styled in a bowl cut, and freckles took over her plump pale face. She slouched over the morning newspaper in her oversized LSU t-shirt and a pair of gym shorts. It looked like I would have a summer project ahead of me with this girl.

"I hope you two are hungry!" Aunt Dee sang as she poured some grease into a frying pan. I could smell the biscuits in the oven and knew that I would definitely have to go for a long run after breakfast to make sure they wouldn't be sticking to my thighs.

"I'm Libby, your cousin by the way." I leaned in toward Brittany.

Brittany sighed, in an annoyed sort of way. "I know."

"Well, I mean, since I'm going to be living here at least for a little while, I figure maybe we could get to know each other. You know, you can like show me around." I twirled a loose strand of hair. I couldn't ruin the only chance with potentially the only person I had to talk to all summer.

Brittany looked up from the newspaper and then back at Aunt Dee who was busy stirring up some gravy with her back to us. Brittany then locked her green eyes on me.

"Alright, look, there's a party tonight at my friend's place. I mean, it's no society party or whatever, but it'll be something to get you out of the house." Her thick Louisiana accent poured out of her chapped lips. She sounded reluctant at first, like she was hoping that I might say no, but then a small smile crept across her face like she maybe had some fate in a future friendship.

"A party?" What kind of party could a fifteen-year-old girl be going to? I mean I guess there had been plenty of people in my high school that could throw some parties. Not that I was ever invited to any. But I remembered almost the entire football team getting suspended for a party that got a bit out of hand in another suburb. So it was entirely plausible that some high school kids in Louisiana might be able to throw something together.

"Shhh." She pursed a short, nubby finger to her lips. "We'll tell Grandma you're going with me to my friend Sarah's, which is half the truth, and she won't know half the difference."

I nodded as Aunt Dee turned toward us with a big pan of jumbo biscuits in her hand. "I am so glad to see you two getting along." She smiled. "Now, who wants breakfast?"

∞

"What to wear. What to wear," I mumbled as I tossed through my clothes, aimlessly throwing them on the floor as I went through my suitcase.

"You know this isn't one of your Chicago parties. It's just more of a t-shirt and jeans type of thing." Brittany chimed in as she leaned against the bed post.

"Yes, but I want to make a good first impression. What do you think all your friends would think if they saw me walk in with what I had on when I met you?" I questioned and looked over a halter top to meet Brittany's gaze.

I spent most of the day getting situated around the house. After I put away my things, I searched the internet for anything that could be remotely entertaining in Elsbury, Louisiana. Needless to say, when the population is only five thousand people there isn't much around for entertainment.

Aunt Dee had told me that she would take me over to the gift shop the next day so that I could start working. The pay would be very minimal, but like she had said, with free room and board I couldn't really complain. I wasn't sure what to expect because it really wasn't like I had ever had to work while I lived at home. Dad was the dentist to most of the professional athletes in Chicago, and sometimes I would help with the filing in his office. That was just about the extent of my work experience.

Mom had always thought that it was more important to concentrate on my school work than to have a job, and the fact that I never had to want for anything. Even while I was in college, my parents paid me an allowance. I found myself always using this money to foot the bill when I went out with my friends at the bar, but it didn't bother me. I was just thankful to have friends and people that at least pretended that they wanted to be around me.

To say that I was privileged was somewhat of an understatement, but I wouldn't exactly say that I had been spoiled growing up. I didn't especially take advantage of the fact that my parents were wealthy, or that I lived in one of the upper-class suburbs of Chicago. Before college I was a nobody.

It wasn't like the football team was knocking down my door to come have a party at my house. When I said I didn't have friends before college, I meant it. So every friend that I made in college mattered. And that's why I actually started to get excited about Brittany's company, which I didn't think would matter to me. I made it my secret mission to give her a full makeover by the end of the summer…even though she spent the whole day refusing to let me pluck her eyebrows.

"Well, they would have asked you to maybe not wear your pants so low that you can see your underwear." She giggled, so I threw the halter top at her.

"Hey! I had just woken up, give me a break!"

"It's not like any of the boys are going to be able to stop gawking at you anyways. A pretty blonde girl from Chicago, you could probably walk in wearing a paper sack and they would be happy." Brittany looked down at her hands as she said that.

I could tell she had some self-esteem issues. She didn't grow up like I did with a mother who had used every wrinkle cream and makeup product ever made. She grew up with Aunt Dee, a woman whose idea of a facial was when she got mud on her face from working in the garden.

"Well, I mean, I'm sure you have to have a boyfriend." I picked up a pair of kitten heels and set them aside. "This town isn't big enough for you not to."

"Well there is this one guy..." She peered out the window.

"Well, tell me about him!" I hit her with a tank top to draw her attention back to me.

"He's not my boyfriend though!" she squealed defensively. "I mean he's probably the hottest guy in the parish, but he's definitely not my boyfriend."

"Well, what's he like?" I pushed. "Will he be there tonight?"

She twiddled her thumbs in her lap. "I guess. He usually doesn't miss a party."

"So we know he's a partier. That could be a good thing." I held up a jean skirt, a possibility, and set it next to the heels.

"Well he's not just a partier. He's your age, and he

already has a job working for the highway department. So he looks really good without his shirt on from working outside all day. Sometimes I make Grandma take the long way home from school just so I can see him."

I smiled as I saw a genuine look of happiness on Brittany's face. She had a crush, but not a crush on any guy I would ever go for. A road crew guy? Ew. But none the less, I was going to try and make her look hot for him at this party tonight.

"Do you have a boyfriend?" she asked after she went on for what seemed like forever about the road crew guy, Blaine, who I could have probably told you his whole life story by then.

"It's kind of on-again, off-again." I bit my lip and sat down on the bed next to Brittany.

"So is he your boyfriend or is he not?" Brittany looked at me for an answer.

That was a hard one to answer. The last time I saw Beau was at school, and we had gotten in a fight because he said he was just helping a Tri-Lambda get something that was caught on her skirt. Of course if that was the case I don't think he would have needed his entire hand up her skirt. But that was Beau. Every time I caught him with another girl it was some kind of an excuse, and then the girl would just run off without saying a word, with her cheeks red as a tomato.

Of course I didn't believe his lies, but I didn't know what else I was supposed to do. He was popular. Something I had always wanted to be. He was an officer in the Alpha Mu fraternity, and probably one of the most well-known guys on campus, and not just for his rugby skills. I knew exactly why I started dating him: instant popularity. Why I stayed with him for so long was a mystery even to me.

I guess I just let the popularity of being the girlfriend of one of the hottest guys on campus get to my head, and I tried my best to ignore his infidelities no matter how much it hurt. But that was over. His project with me was done. He would soon find another girl to be his arm candy. As he put it, "We had fun Libby. But it's better to go off on a good note." That was the last thing he said to me, as I was almost in tears when I called him to let him know I was leaving for Louisiana.

No sense of sympathy, not even empathy, it was like he was just bored with the conversation. Soon after, he broke up with me, and he told me he had to go because he was really busy. I knew that it was probably because he had a girl with him, or at least someone. He was the last person I expected to spend the night alone.

"Well, I guess for now I am single and free." I beamed. "Maybe your Blaine boy has a friend for me." I winked, almost convincing myself that maybe I would meet someone too, but I thought that would never happen. Even though I had only had one boyfriend in my life, from what I saw of the locals I wasn't going to find the type of guy I normally went for. I saw these guys walking down the block, wearing trucker caps, while walking their hunting dogs. I wasn't even sure I was ready to put myself out there, just to get let down again.

CHAPTER 5

"What are you so dressed up for?"

Aunt Dee looked up at me with her glasses brimming on her nose. I didn't think I was too dressed up, at least not for me, just a white lace tank top, jean skirt, and a pair of black kitten heels.

"Well, I have to make a good impression on the locals, don't I?" I strutted down the little carpet runner to the couch where Aunt Dee was. I had tried to get Brittany to wear something a little nicer or even put on some makeup, but she said she was fine in a lime green cut off shirt and gym shorts. I was going to burn those gym shorts by the end of the summer.

"I told her she was too dressed up to just go hang out at Sarah's, but you know them blondes, Aunt Dee." They shared a laugh and I glared at the two of them.

"And you are going to walk to Sarah's trailer in those heels?" Aunt Dee gawked down at my feet...and I was pretty sure she had just said trailer...gulp.

"Grandma!" Brittany bellowed. "I walk to Sarah's all the time, and it ain't that far!"

"Well you've never walked in heels." Aunt Dee got up from the couch and walked over to the kitchen. "In fact." She reached into her purse. "I don't think I've ever seen you in anything close to heels." Aunt Dee threw me a set of keys.

"Here, I ain't letting you walk all the way to Sarah's like that. You never know what kind of hooligans are out." Aunt Dee smiled at me as I looked down at the keys.

"Gee, thanks Aunt Dee..."

Brittany beamed and jumped up, taking me by the arm as she led me out the door. "Bye Grandma, we won't be home too late. Just watching movies and stuff," she called as we headed out the door. Somehow I think I knew then that this was definitely not going to be like any other party that I had ever been to.

∞

When we arrived it became clear that this was definitely not a Chicago party, or even a college party for that matter. I pulled the car up to a rusted trailer with some terrible music that I didn't recognize, blasting from inside. I turned off the ignition and looked over at Brittany.

"Are you sure this is a good idea? I mean, Aunt Dee does trust us," I said.

I couldn't believe I was being the sensible one. Usually I was the one begging the girls in my house to go out, the girl that was always looking for a good time, but for some reason I was getting knots in my stomach.

It wasn't like I didn't go to a lot of parties in college or anything, but this one just felt different to me. At the time, I thought it was just the atmosphere. I had never set foot in a trailer or a swamp until that night, and I couldn't concentrate on anything else but the bowed out double-wide and how much my heels were sinking in the ground.

"Yeah, yeah I do it all the time." Brittany unbuckled her seat belt and jumped out of the car.

We walked past the gawkers on the rickety front porch and inside to the smoky house. Brittany was definitely right; this was a t-shirt and jeans party. Or more like cut-off shirts and shorts party, and I definitely stuck out like a sore thumb.

"Hey you made it!" A very hefty blonde ran over to Brittany and gave her a big squeeze.

"And you must be Libby. I'm Sarah!" The girl's accent could have rivaled Patsy Cline, but I was too busy being enveloped in her big arms to pay too much attention.

"Why you are just as pretty as Dee said you would be!"

I could feel the heat rising in my face. It wasn't like I didn't get a lot of attention at school, but sometimes it could be a little too much.

Sarah looked behind her and then back at Brittany and she leaned in to the two of us. "Blaine is here," she whispered, giggling after she said it.

I put my hands on Brittany's shoulder. "Aw, you hear that? You should go talk to him!"

"No. I ain't going to go talk to him. He don't even know who I am," Brittany mumbled, crossing her arms across her huge chest.

"Of course he knows who you are, there are only five-thousand people in this town!" I exclaimed. "Now, where is he?" I let my eyes scan the room. It was packed with boys chewing tobacco and girls wearing cowboy hats. Brittany pointed toward the couch.

"That one, sitting in the middle."

That's when I caught my first glimpse of Blaine Crabtree. He was sandwiched in between two guys that were laughing at who knows what. At first I didn't notice anything but a big mop of bleached blonde hair, then he looked up from his pack of cloves and I was locked into the bluest eyes that I had ever seen. His expression didn't change, he didn't smile and didn't blink. It seemed like I was lost in his eyes, like he was using them to do the most calculated math problem, and that math problem was me.

I quickly gathered myself as best as I could and looked down, trying to hide my smile by biting down on my lower lip. I had hoped that no one was watching, but obviously someone else noticed our stare-down.

"What was that all about?" Sarah teased. "You better watch your man." Sarah poked Brittany in the ribs. Brittany was not amused, and looked just about as embarrassed as I was, not taking her eyes off of the ground.

I tilted my head up. "Well I guess we will just have to make him notice Brittany then!" They looked puzzled as I headed over to the stereo with the girls closely following behind me, whispering back and forth.

I crouched down and rummaged through the pile of CDs next to the stereo system. Tool? Really? Nine Inch Nails? It was no wonder everyone was just standing around. Finally I found something that would work with my plan, a disc of Def Leppard's greatest hits. I opened the CD case and put the disc into the stereo.

Everyone around me stopped what they were doing and grumbled, looking at me. I heard snippets of conversation in hushed tones, what the hell is she doing? Then, "Pour Some Sugar on Me" started playing and I turned toward Brittany.

"Come on!" I reached my arms out to her, slowly swaying my hips as I stood up.

"Come on what?" She firmly crossed her arms across her chest.

I tugged on her arms and kept swaying, sliding my body up and down. She wouldn't budge, her arms were glued around her shirt and kept her eyes locked on the ground.

"If you want Blaine to notice you, dance with me."

"I don't dance." She looked around and her cheeks flushed.

"You don't need to know how to dance. It's all basically just dry humping anyways!" I slid my body down to a crouching position in front of her and then slowly popped back up, sticking my butt out.

"I choreographed Kappa Beta's spring Dance Off, Pants Off. I can show you some moves." I tried to pull on her arms again, swaying my body around her, and tried to lift her arms over her head. I leaned my back against her and slid down, as if she were a pole, and then slowly popped back up swinging my hair. She looked away from me and darted toward the other end of the room with Sarah following close behind.

"Britt! Wait!" I yelled and turned on my heels to go toward her, but a tight grip pulled me back.

"What the hell do you think you're doing?" A deep country accent growled behind me. I turned toward the vice grip owner and met those blue eyes again.

"What the hell do you think YOU are doing?" I tried to pull my arm away, but this guy had a stronger grip than I thought.

"Come on outside and talk to me," he whispered motioning his head toward the door.

"I will do no such thing!" I tried to pull my arm away, but he had a grip that could only come from hours of manual labor and it was no use trying to break it. He pulled me toward the door with him, and we had caused quite the scene. We exited to the front porch where people stood gawking at us.

"Who do you think you are, my father?" I hissed turning toward him, my hair flying about.

"No, but I'm not going to let some guy take advantage of you in there." He let go of my arm and reached in his pocket, pulling out a pack of cloves. He leaned against the porch railing like he was just making himself at home.

I crossed my arms and smirked. "I think I can handle myself. I took a self-defense class during Greek Week."

He placed a clove between his lips, letting out a muffled laugh while he lit it. "Yeah, at the college you failed out of."

"Hey now, you probably don't even go to college, so you have no room to judge!" I pouted.

He exhaled the smoke through his nose and I could hear the crackle of the clove as he removed it from his lips. "Well, no, I didn't go to college. But neither did your Aunt Dee and she's a good lady. I'm not going to let her hear about her niece getting taken advantage of at one of Sarah's parties. She's too good for that."

He took another drag of his clove and his gaze met mine again. I wanted to say something, but his gorgeous blue eyes had me stammering for words. I tried to focus on something else, so that I could regain my words.

I looked down to his shirt, which was nothing special, a plain black shirt. But as I watched, his arm muscles would flinch when he would move his hands from his clove, to the porch, and in and out of the pockets of his faded cargo shorts. I realized how much I was actually focusing on the curves of his body and tried everything I could not to wonder what it was like to be that clove between his lips.

I wasn't too sure what to say to him and I figured that he must have thought I was staring, which in all honesty I was. All I could come up with was that we hadn't officially met, so I changed the subject real quick.

"I'm Libby by the way, but I guess you already knew that." I shifted from one leg to the other.

"Yeah." He exhaled. "When you live in a small town you kind of hear all the news, and my mom is a hairdresser, so I do hear all of the gossip."

"If your mom was a better hairdresser she wouldn't let you bleach your hair."

His hair was so spikey and tousled that it almost looked curly or windblown. I wondered what it would be like to run my fingers through it. If it would feel like straw from baking in the summer sun all day or if it would just slide like silk through my fingers.

"And that really didn't give me any information

about you. If you're going to man handle me, I should at least know your name. And if you plan on doing it again you should really get me a drink first."

He laughed, exhaling a mouthful of smoke. His full lips almost made an O shape as he laughed, bringing out the dimples that curved around his lip line. "Alright, you got me there. I'm Blaine. Blaine who's lived here all his life. Blaine the grunt for the parish highway department."

"Well I didn't want your whole life story!" I squealed. I was flirting. I couldn't help it, and he really was cute in an old faded blue jeans sort of way.

I didn't think that I would ever date a guy from Elsbury. He probably spent all day working and then going home to watch car racing. He probably drove a big red truck and blared Charlie Daniels. A guy like Blaine just didn't fit the description of guys that I was normally attracted to, but with every lingering gaze I found myself wanting to know more about this southern boy.

"Yeah, well that ain't the half of it." He stopped and finished his clove. I thought he was going to say something more, but then he looked all around us. "Hey, where did your cousin go?"

"Hmm..? Oh, Brittany? I'm sure she is fine." I waved my hand in front of me before letting it fall flat.

"You really are dense aren't you?" He flicked his clove off of the porch, narrowing his eyes at me before he walked back inside with long, quick strides.

I stormed after him, pushing past plaid shirted guys and tube top clad girls. "What the hell? You're the one that dragged me outside remember?" I turned

Blaine toward me as we got into the living room, trying to ignore how toned his biceps were. I had to resist the urge to trace my fingers down them.

"You leave a fifteen-year-old girl alone at a party and expect everything is just going to be alright?" He raised his voice. I didn't like being told what I should be doing or being questioned by a guy I barely knew. Especially a guy that had dragged me outside when I was trying to chase after Britt in the first place.

"I'm sure she's fine, I mean she's the one who invited me to this party!" I threw an arm out to the side. "And if it's so bad, then why are you here?" I crossed my arms and smirked, trying to make my point.

"Because I am a nineteen-year-old man, not a fifteen-year-old girl whose cousin just used her like a stripper pole!" He screamed that last part, and headed off toward one of the bedrooms. Everyone was staring at us. I put my head down and tried not to let everyone see how red I'm sure my face was as I hurried to catch up with Blaine.

I caught up to him standing in an open doorway, and staring as he leaned in on the door frame. A small crowd of people were positioned in the room lit by only black lights and cluttered with posters of psychedelic pink mushrooms and other brightly colored plants. As the cloud of smoke lifted I saw my little cousin, curled up on the corner of an old wooden futon with a plastic cup in one hand and her mouth wrapped around a giant green bong that was being lit by some guy with a porn star mustache. I gasped, covering my own mouth in horror.

"Real responsible aren't we?" Blaine whispered as

he headed back out toward the party.

"Hey cuz!" Brittany giggled, letting out a huge cloud of smoke. "Want a hit?" She held out the large green bong toward me. I had never smoked pot and never planned to, but I wasn't a stranger to it. It wasn't like a lot of Beau's fraternity brothers didn't spend their time hitting the bong.

I threw my arms down and stomped over to Brittany. "No I do not want a hit! We are leaving!" I pulled her up off the couch, it was like pulling dead weight, but I managed to get her up.

"Come on girl! The party is just getting started, and I got a spot for you right here." I looked down to see a Hispanic boy in a cowboy hat wiping his mouth, suggesting that I should sit on it.

"Ew..." I wrinkled my nose in disgust and pulled Brittany out of the room.

"Oh come on cuz, we were just having some fun!" Brittany laughed as she chugged the contents of the cup down and then threw the empty cup on the ground. She then turned to me with a serious glint in her bloodshot eyes.

"You were probably having fun with Blaine anyways!" She pointed at me, staggering back and forth.

"Trust me Britt. There is NOTHING going on with me and Blaine. I don't think there is going to be any luck with guys for me in this entire parish." I gritted as I pulled her toward the door.

"Where do you think y'all are going?" Blaine forced himself in front of us in the door way. He appeared out of nowhere. I stopped cold and narrowed my eyes.

"I am taking my baby cousin home, DAD," I spat.

Brittany giggled. She was high as a kite and smelled like oregano and cheap vodka. I tried to go around Blaine, but he just darted in front of me again.

"Do you even know how to get home?" Blaine gave a smug smirk like he actually had some satisfaction in knowing that I needed his help.

"Well, I'm sure I can find my way, Brittany can help!" By this time Brittany was completely engrossed at staring at a clock on the wall. It became clear that my little GPS had screwed me over.

"C'mon, I'll take you two in my truck," Blaine said, putting his hand out toward me and widening his eyes. I smacked his hand away.

"You will do no such thing! I have Aunt Dee's car here, and I can't just leave it!"

He sighed, thrusting his hand into his pocket. "Fine, then I'll drive my truck and you two can follow me. Once I see that you get in the house I'll leave. Fair enough?"

I looked over at Brittany. There was no way that she was coherent enough to tell me the directions. The trailer was so far out in the middle of nowhere, that I knew I couldn't get back to Aunt Dee's by myself.

"Fine, let's go." I pushed passed Blaine and out to the sticky Louisiana summer air.

∞

Following a big, red pickup truck through swamp land in Aunt Dee's old Grand Am with a high and drunk fifteen-year-old in the passenger seat was not my ideal way to spend my first weekend in Elsbury.

It was so dark outside and the mist was so thick, that I could barely see anything, except for Blaine's bright yellow union bumper sticker.

"Would it really kill the highway department to put up some street lights?" I grumbled, turning on my wipers and hoping that would have made a difference in the fog. It didn't.

Brittany laughed like I just said the funniest thing ever. She had been laughing at everything I said. It was getting really annoying.

"Whoa, I think Blaine just turned." Brittany slowly pointed a chubby finger out the front window.

"Shit.

I missed him turning while I was trying to focus on Brittany. I did a quick U-turn loop down into a gravel path. The tires squealed underneath me. I knew there was a reason that Pontiac went out of business. The car sputtered and squealed as I finished the turn, but I wasn't out of the woods just yet. In my rear view mirror I saw the red and blue lights.

I had an underage girl that was definitely under the influence and I was driving a car that wasn't mine. All I could think about was that maybe a fast food job would have been better than jail. I pulled the car over and waited for the police officer to come up to the car.

"You know, the last time I saw my mom she was out here. Maybe her spirit can come back and help us!" Brittany gestured out the door as she pressed her nose to the glass.

I tried to ignore her as I went through my mind as to what I would say to the cops. The truth? Sorry officer I am driving my high fifteen-year-old cousin home, who only got high because I was busy getting assaulted by her man candy?

Yeah, I'm sure that would work real well. Before I could even have another thought, Brittany had darted out the door and toward the wooded area beside the road.

"Shit!" I bolted out of the door as fast as I could, not even looking back to see if the cop was following me.

"Mama! Mama! I know you're out here! Mama!" Brittany cupped her hands over her mouth like a makeshift megaphone.

Before I could reach Brittany, Blaine had bolted out in front of me and grabbed her. I was surprised to see him since I thought he had long passed me. He held Brittany by both shoulders and turned her toward him, looking into her face.

"Brittany, now you know your mama ain't out here. Her spirit is up in heaven, not in the swamp." Brittany looked at him with tears in her bloodshot eyes.

"She has to be! This is the spot I last saw her! Remember, before she got arrested!" Brittany screamed almost choking on her tears. Blaine held Brittany close to him as her tears and muffled words soaked through his shirt.

Blaine nodded toward me as I felt a hand on my shoulder. I turned my head back to see the cop with his eyes tapered and his lips formed a tight line as he stared right at me.

I bit my lip. "Um...I wish I could say I can explain." I sighed. "But I can't and I'm sorry." I put my wrists out toward the cop. "Go on, take me in."

The cop started laughing uncontrollably, spit forming at the sides of his mouth and lingering on his mustache. "Do you really think I'm going to take you in?"

I tilted my head. "Um...what?"

"Look, I pulled you over because of that illegal U-turn, but it's not like I'm going to take you into jail. Is that what they do in Chicago?" The cop laughed again, especially at the word Chicago like he had made some hilarious joke at my expense.

"Look." He put his hand on my shoulder. "This isn't the first time something like this has happened with Brittany, and what your aunt don't know won't hurt her."

I looked over my shoulder at Blaine rubbing Brittany's back as they walked toward us. I tried to hide a longing smile. Beau would have never done anything like that for me, or anyone else for that matter. When his little brother broke his arm, he used his cast to rest his beer on. Blaine was doing just the opposite, putting someone else before himself and it was hard for me to stay mad at him. No matter how hard I was trying to maintain a serious disposition.

"Blaine told me what was going on, and don't worry. Dee may be good on the town gossip, but what she don't know won't hurt her." The cop said as I turned my attention back toward him.

I smiled weakly. I didn't know if he was just a dirty cop that Blaine paid off, or maybe this was just how people took care of each other in small towns. Either way I was afraid that if things were like this all the time I would have a heart attack before the end of the summer.

"Let's get you two home," Blaine said. He patted me gently on the back with his free hand, his other arm still protectively around Brittany. I couldn't help but lean in closer to him as we approached the car. I wondered what was really going through his mind and how this guy could appear to be such a hard ass, but yet would go out of his way to help someone.

The cop left and I got Brittany back in the car. Blaine's eyes seemed to never leave our car. Even through the mist it seemed like I could see nothing but the blue of his eyes and trusted that he would help us find our way home.

Finally, after what seemed like hours but was only minutes, we pulled into Aunt Dee's carport.

"You better go inside and wash up before Dee gets a smell of you." Blaine called to Brittany as she got out of the car. She nodded and ran toward the front porch. I couldn't tell if she was embarrassed or just coming down from her high.

"I don't know if I should be pissed at you or thank you." I put my hands on either side of my hips as I leaned back against the car.

"Well if you would have been watching your cousin, or even the road, maybe none of this would have happened." Suddenly that soft disposition was gone and only the hard exterior remained.

"Maybe if you weren't trying to grope me at the party we wouldn't have this problem!" I hissed.

He laughed. "Me? Trying to grope you?"

"What's so damn funny?" I dug my heel into the ground.

"Well, no offense darling." He ran his fingers through his hair. "But you're not really my type. A little too high maintenance for me.

Alright so maybe there wasn't any sort of a soft disposition. This boy was just infuriating. "Then why even care? Why even bother with talking to me at the party?"

"Look, like I told you, your Aunt Dee is a good lady and so is Brittany. I'm not going to let something happen to their family, and I'm not going to let Aunt Dee find out about anything that happened tonight."

I prodded him in the stomach with my index finger. "Look here Blaine. You are not my father and you are not the keeper of my aunt's family. So just stay out of my life and I will do the same for you!" Before he could respond I turned and stormed into the house, shutting the door as quietly as I could behind me even though I just wanted to slam it right in Blaine's face.

I watched Blaine from the front window. He stood there, shaking his head as a dimpled smirk crossed his lips. He finally got into his truck and pulled out of the driveway.

I was an entire melting pot of emotions: confused, enraged, and well…kind of intrigued all at the same time. I didn't know if that would be the last that I would see of Blaine and part of me was hoping that it would be. Another part, a small part, was hoping that it wouldn't be.

CHAPTER 6

I could usually sleep in with no problem, but Aunt Dee's food was not something you could sleep through. The smell of pancakes reached my nose as soon as I woke up, and I was throwing that pink marshmallow comforter off of my bed faster than I knew I could, to scamper into the kitchen.

My brown eyes searched the kitchen. Aunt Dee was over the stove flipping pancakes, but Brittany wasn't at the table.

"Morning Aunt Dee. Where's Britt?" I stretched my arms over my head, before leaning over the counter top.

Aunt Dee pushed up her glasses with the palm of her hand as she looked up at me. "Oh she's still sleeping." She looked back down at the pancakes. "Poor thing must be tired out. It's been a busy week for her; new woman in the house, school ending, and lots of new things."

I nodded. I thought it would be a good chance for Aunt Dee and me to talk. What happened last night was definitely weird. Not just the party, but I couldn't imagine why Brittany would run out into the woods after her mom. From what I'd known of her mom it didn't seem like she was a good person. And if her mom was dead, why would she be looking for her?

But I was trying to remain unsuspicious.

"Hey, Aunt Dee?"

"Yes honey?" She prodded at the pancakes. I was almost drooling as I watched them bubble before she flipped them onto a plate.

"Has Britt's mom not been around for a while?"

Aunt Dee had a puzzled look on her face, like she was thinking really deep. She carried the plate of pancakes over to the table and gestured for me to follow.

"Well what makes you ask a question like that, honey?" She scooped two pancakes onto my plate and one onto hers before sitting down.

"Oh just curious, I mean, gosh, being fifteen it would have been weird not seeing my mom every day." I was really curious as to why Brittany would be looking for her mom in the woods, and hoped not to make it too obvious.

Aunt Dee looked over my shoulder, nodding, I guess she was making sure Brittany's door was closed.

"Well," she whispered. "The last time I can remember Brittany seeing her mom, before she passed, was kind of..." She stopped, like she was searching for the right words. "Well, it wasn't pretty."

"How so?" I doused my pancakes in syrup, only looking down briefly before returning my attention back to Aunt Dee.

"Joni was never the most trustworthy person, and she sure knew how to take advantage of people." Aunt Dee put a napkin on her lap.

"It was a few years ago, she told me she wanted to start seeing Brittany again, and that was something I sure wasn't happy about. And I told her that." She started cutting her pancakes into tiny little bites. "Joni didn't take no for an answer either."

She plopped a piece of pancake into her mouth, and kept on proceeding with the story as bits of pancake came out of her teeth as she spoke. I was too engrossed in the story at this point to really care that she was practically spitting on me. My mother would have probably said something at this point, but I wasn't about to stop her. For one thing I didn't want to hurt her feelings, and for another thing I wanted to hear the story.

"She was staying with some guy off Old Conger Road and started meeting Brittany in the woods over by there."

"So Brittany was meeting up with her in the woods?" I rested my chin in my palm and leaned forward to get a better listen.

"Yes of all places! As it turns out Joni was just looking for money as always. Told Brittany she wanted to see her, but was always having her bring money." Aunt Dee wiped her mouth. "It started out with Brittany just emptying her piggy bank, but when that wasn't enough she started taking money from me…"

"How much money?" I wondered if I was being too forward, but I remembered how open Aunt Dee was when I first met her, and thought she would trust me enough to tell me the details.

She looked down. "Within about six months I almost lost the house, since Brittany had taken almost everything from my checking and savings."

My mouth gaped open. I couldn't believe it. "Oh

my God! Aunt Dee!"

"Shh!" She put a finger to her lips and pointed at Brittany's door. "And don't use the Lord's name in vain." She tapped my hand, meaning for it to come out like a slap on the wrist. I don't think she really wanted to hurt me.

"Oh sorry..." I whispered. "Well, what did you do?"

"The only thing I could do. Even though she was my daughter. I had to get the police involved." She sighed. "However, Joni ended up running away again, with all of our money. She left poor Brittany trying to go back to those dang woods for weeks to try and find her. Brittany even believed she could still talk to her there after she passed."

"What did you do about the money then?" I pondered between bites of food.

"Well, I had to cash out some old stocks and bonds, but we ended up being alright. Don't you worry about me Libby." She patted my free hand. "We are just fine."

I popped another bite of pancake in my mouth as Aunt Dee and I sat in silence. You could hear every scrape of our forks as we cleaned our plates. Brittany still was not up yet, and my stomach was feeling bloated. I had consumed more carbs in my two days in Louisiana than I had my entire freshman year of college.

"Hey Aunt Dee?" I leaned in on the table as she started clearing our plates.

"Yes dear?" She took a sponge to her plate, not looking up from the sink as she spoke.

"I think I am going to go for a run before work. Is

that alright? I promise I won't be too long." My thighs could really use it.

"Why sure honey, go right ahead. I'll clean up here and when you get back we can head on over to the paper." She looked up and smiled at me through those Coke bottle glasses. I had only known this woman a few days, but I already knew why Blaine and everyone seemed to like her so much.

∞

I used to run every day in college. I prided myself on being one of the only girls in my dorm that actually lost weight instead of gaining the freshman fifteen. Some say they chalked it up to the fact that when you are in the spotlight all the time, or just a new sorority pledge, forces you into the binge, purge, and run habit. My parents thought all my troubles at school were drinking and partying with my sorority sisters.

They never really paid attention to why the water was always running when I was in the bathroom, or how I was missing class because I just HAD to stay up to be the designated driver for the older members with the rest of my pledge class.

All these thoughts crossed my mind as I got dressed for my run. I so badly wanted to just put on an oversized tee shirt and some sweat pants to run, I could just feel my pants getting tighter, but it was just too hot. I put on a sports bra and a pair of yoga pants, at least with them being black it had a slimming affect. I strapped my iPod on my armband and put in my earbuds to be surrounded by the sounds of pop music. It was a nice break from Brittany's weird rock music or Aunt Dee's twangy country music.

At eight in the morning it was probably already about ninety degrees. I was glad that I put my hair up because I could already feel the sweat dripping down my neck. I thought I would do just a mile or two and run down to the end of Aunt Dee's street and back. Which was a pretty long way. I was focused on my music and the road ahead of me, the lyrics filling my ears.

Finally getting to see Elsbury in the daytime, it looked a lot different than what I was expecting. In high school we had to watch Gone with the Wind, so I was expecting that every southern town looked like Civil War era Atlanta. Needless to say, Elsbury was nothing like that and Tara wasn't anywhere in site.

Even though it had been years since a hurricane went through, parts of the town looked like they just had a recent storm. I passed dozens of houses with big orange X's on the door and there were even some areas where it was nothing but cement stairs. I'm sure the stairs used to lead right up to the front porches of someone's home, but now it was just these random stairs to nowhere. I felt like it was kind of a metaphor for my past year. Each step was a different path I took my freshman year of college and where did that lead me? Nowhere.

After getting lost in my own thoughts, I snapped out of it when I heard something to the right of me. Out of the corner of my eye I saw some guys working on a road crew in front of a white house off of a little side street. Their bright orange vests could have blinded anyone, and since they were standing in front of some big, yellow machines I don't think I could have missed them.

"Damn if I would have known they made girls this good looking I would have moved to this Parrish a long time ago." A very tan Cajun-looking man whistled.

Two other guys nodded along with him, as they looked over whatever giant road equipment they had. Then I saw him out of the corner of my eye, it was Blaine, the last person I really wanted to see.

At first he didn't notice it was me, but when he did his blue eyes got wide. I smiled and turned away from him, giving a wink to the other three guys as they whistled and shouted some pretty graphic things. I beamed thinking maybe those pancakes weren't sticking to my thighs, but then I was taken back to reality as I felt Mr. Vice Grip yank me back.

"Hey!" I stopped and pulled out my ear buds as I glared at Blaine. "What was that all about?"

"What the hell is wrong with you?" I couldn't tell if he was narrowing his eyes at me, or if he was just squinting from the sun, but either way I could tell he was not happy.

"What the hell is wrong with me?" I blew a stray strand of hair out of my eyes. "What the hell is wrong with you? You can't just go around grabbing girls all the time. That is not how you make friends!" I pushed his arm off of me.

"Well do you think you are really going to be meeting people running around half-naked and hitting on road crew guys?" He crossed his arms over his chest, the veins bulging from his muscular arms. I had to snap my head away from them so I would stop staring.

"Aren't you a road crew worker?" I tilted my head.
"That's not the point."

I smirked. No matter how built he was, and how much I wanted to stare into those blue eyes, this guy was really pissing me off. I don't know where he got off always telling me what to do, but it was really getting irritating.

"Then what is the point Blaine? That you like to tell me what to do? That you seem to get off on trying to stop me from what little bit of fun I am having in this stupid town?"

He opened his mouth to say something, but I stopped him before he could speak.

"No. Just stop it Blaine. Let's get something straight here." I poked my index finger at his chest. "You are NOT my father, you are NOT my family's keeper, and you are NOT my boyfriend. Hell, you are not even my friend. So stop acting like it's your duty to protect me from whatever danger I am in, and just leave me alone!"

I turned away from him and started almost sprinting back to my aunt's. I wanted to look back, but I knew if I did I might do something drastic. Like punch him right in those stupid blue eyes.

CHAPTER 7

Aunt Dee's antique shop looked like someone just threw a bunch of stuff from their attic in an abandoned warehouse. Mom used to take me into these old, quaint antique shops near Galena that contained pretty china and old paintings on the wall, but Aunt Dee's place had none of these. Unless they were hidden underneath one of the rows of old oil cans that lined the walls.

The shop was located on what would be called the "down town" I didn't know that a downtown could consist of a post office, fire department, one bar, and one restaurant, and that was the big draws. That was the signature downtown…about three city block's worth of entertainment.

The first time I went into the shop it was like I was some sort of circus freak. I thought I should dress up since it was my first day of work, and so I wore my black pants suit, my mom insisted that I bought one when I graduated from high school.

She also thought it would be a great work outfit for me this summer. Well, it looked like I was the only one that was dressed up. I guess my mom didn't account for the heat, that always seems to leave you covered in a fine mist no matter how long you've been outside, or that people don't really wear suits when you work at an antique shop.

The main are wasn't that much bigger than one of my college classrooms. The walls wooden walls were lined with shelves containing dusty pottery and rusted, metal signs were plastered to the walls.

An older woman with salt and pepper hair sat in front of a giant rusted fan, at the front counter, fanning her chicken arms that hung out of a sleeveless, ketchup stained shirt. The other women at the counter looked about mid-thirties and gawked at me from behind her crooked glasses and cheap lip gloss.

The back of the shop contained one closed-off office that was Aunt Dee's, and another small desk sat across from the office that was going to be mine. It definitely wasn't anything fancy, a large metal desk and an overstuffed, green, fake leather chair, which was probably bought from an Army surplus store, but it was a desk. It was a job, and I really couldn't complain too much. It could have been a whole lot worse. I could be in a hairnet.

I had decided to go to school for fashion merchandising. I had always loved fashion and always dressed pretty well. Honestly I would have rather picked another major, but when you're blonde, in a sorority, and your ACT score was only an 18, you weren't really cut out for too much. So I thought fashion merchandising would be easy, I was wrong.

It was hard to concentrate as it was when I was always up either doing something for Kappa or spending a late night at the gym. I couldn't make it to half of my Gen Eds, and my major classes...forget about it. Who knew so much math was involved in fashion? And I felt like I wasn't going to understand it by reading it over and over in my $150 text book.

My teachers really didn't believe in me, and my sorority made me the token blonde ditz. It seemed like Aunt Dee was the only one to actually believe in me. She didn't send me out to work on sorting through the new shipments that came in off the back of some guy's truck. She actually sat me down and taught me how to do the books, I was going to be doing the shop's accounting. I wasn't the dumb blonde holding up the car wash sign, I was the bookkeeper, and it was the first time I had felt proud of myself in a long time.

CHAPTER 8

My learning process was a slow process. Marion (chicken arms) and Dina (snaggletooth) frequently got frustrated with me. But Aunt Dee would just come out of her office, smile, and show me exactly what I did wrong and exactly how to fix it, until everything was balanced. After a week I felt like I was actually doing something worthwhile.

And coincidently it had also been a week since my run-in with Blaine. It wasn't that I wasn't thinking about him, and believe me I was, I wish I could get him out of my head. For some reason he was really getting to me. Brittany would constantly talk about how he hadn't been around Sarah's every time I would see her at dinner. In response, I would just nod and smile.

It was a typical day at the office; Marion was standing over the fan and constantly complaining about how hot she was, instead of doing whatever she was supposed to be doing. Dina was watching random videos on the internet and constantly applying lip-gloss (I guess that's what the sales manager does?).

I sat in my chair, twirling my ponytail, as I kept trying to figure out how we could be missing a random two dollars from the petty cash account, when I heard the bell on the front door ring. I expected it was another customer looking for some old broken teapot. But this person was not a customer, and was enough to take away both Marion and Dina's attention. I could hear them both swoon.

"Hey Blaine." Dina purred.

Blaine? My head popped up. What was he doing here? I was guessing to suck up to Aunt Dee some more, or hell, maybe he was banging Dina. I went back to working on the books as Dina went on and on.

"Are those flowers for me?" She giggled.

Flowers?

"Um..." Blaine stammered. "Actually, I'm here to see Libby."

Me? I kept my eyes down on the books; if he could go a week without an apology then he didn't deserve my attention. But flowers are always nice…

"Oh." Dina smacked her big overly-glossed lips together. "Well, you can see she's in the back." She nodded her head of messy curls over in my direction. I pretended not to notice as Blaine's work boots creaked on the old wooden floor.

"Um…hey…" He was standing right in front of my desk, a pathetic display of carnations that he probably picked up at the gas station in his hands. The red and white of the flowers sharply contrasted against his bright orange work vest.

I glanced up and blew away a stray blonde hair. "Hey." I went back to looking down at the books.

"Um..." He rubbed the back of his neck. "I brought you these."

I put my pencil down on the desk and folded my

hands in front of me as I looked up. "Gee, Blaine first you insult me, then you don't talk to me for a week, and now you come with cheap flowers?" I let out a single laugh.

"Wow, you really know how to impress a girl." That last statement dripped with sarcasm, and by that time we had the attention of the two gossip mongers in the front, and possibly some of the customers milling around the store.

"Look." Blaine leaned in as he lowered his voice. "I'm sorry Libby. I think we got off on the wrong foot". He placed the bouquet on the desk and set both his hands down in front of him, so he could have more leverage to lean in.

"The wrong foot?" I cocked an eyebrow. "You basically called me a slut." I started putting my fingers up to count. "Um, I believe stupid." I put another finger up. "Oh, and a horrible niece and cousin." I put that last finger up with a sense of defiance. "Did I miss anything else?"

He sighed. "Look, Libby." I could almost see the sweat form on his brow. "I am sorry for all of that. I never really gave you a chance and I should have. You've been the talk of the town these past two weeks and no one has got anything bad to say about you."

"Go on." I rested my chin in my hand and leaned in closer. Our foreheads were less than a foot apart now.

"Well, I think I should make it up to you, and I thought maybe I could take you to dinner tonight. Your choice of the place." He cracked a nervous smile. I could tell it was a nervous smile because it was almost too toothy. He did have perfect teeth though, I noticed. It was like he had years of braces. As a dentist's daughter I noticed these things. I also really paid attention, since I expected him to be missing a few teeth, but I think that was just me stereotyping.

"Hmm." I tapped my nails on my chin and looked toward the ceiling. "I don't know. You were awfully mean." I then looked back at him and let an almost Cheshire-like smile cross my lips.

"Aw come on Libby. Don't play it like that." His southern accent got thicker, and a little bit more playful as he leaned in even closer. We were only inches apart now.

I let out a sarcastic sigh. "Okay, but just this once."

He grinned, "Can I pick you up tonight around six then?"

"No." I slowly shook my head. "I'm busy. Its bridge club night, so I'm staying home with Britt."

"Okay. Fine how about tomorrow?" That nervous sweat was beginning to form again.

"I think there is a new TV show on that night."

"Oh come on!" He was visibly getting frustrated now as he balled his hands into fist.

"I can do Friday." I bit my lower lip teasingly and looked up at him.

"Finally." He sighed. "I'll pick you up at six on Friday then?"

"Sounds good." I beamed. We were practically close enough to be kissing, but then he looked over and saw the two ladies pretending not to stare.

He coughed, covering his mouth with his hand as he straightened himself. "Well I guess I should be getting back to work."

"Oh yeah, definitely, someone has to work on those roads." I nodded and realized I sounded like an idiot.

"Alright Libby. I'll see you Friday." He smiled and nodded to the two ladies in front as he walked out the front door.

No sooner had he left, he wasn't even out of sight of the front windows yet, when Dina and Marion came running over to my desk.

"Looks like someone is getting some on Friday!" Marion giggled shaking her enormous saggy breasts in front of my desk.

"With Blaine?" I furrowed my brow. "No, it's not like that." The truth was, Beau was the only guy I had ever slept with, and I definitely was not going to give it up that easy again.

"Well Blaine IS like that." Dina smirked.

"What do you mean?" I cocked my head. For the guy that was concerned about me running in a sports bra, he didn't seem like the screw-on-the-first-date type.

"Well." Marion chimed. "He has kind of always been the playboy type. I think every woman under the age of thirty has crossed his path at least once."

"Including me." Dina beamed. "But that was like six months ago. If you want him you can have him." She aimlessly tossed a pale hand in the air like she was swatting a fly.

Ew. Blaine and Dina with the Lee Press-on Nails and orthopedic shoes, gross. And who was Blaine to tell me that I was acting like a skank when he was banging half the town? Well, our Friday night was sure going to be interesting.

CHAPTER 9

"Are these jeans too tight?"

I faced my butt in the direction of Britt, who was sitting Indian style on my bed. She wasn't happy about Blaine taking me out, but changed her spirits as soon as she found out that I was not into it.

"I don't know. I really don't want to look at your butt." Britt laughed.

"Well, I've been eating too much of Aunt Dee's cooking and I'm afraid all my clothes are looking tight and not in the good way." It was true. My clothes were getting a lot tighter, and I didn't want Blaine to think I was wearing tight pants just for his attention.

"Okay then." I lifted up a t-shirt to my chest. "How about this?"

"Peace, Love, Kappa?" Britt raised an eyebrow at the faded green ringer tee.

"Yeah, it was given to me by an alum. I think the old and wornness of it definitely says: Blaine I am not doing you." I nodded.

"So why are you even going on a date with him if you don't have any interest in him? I mean, if you really didn't want to go out with him you could have thrown him my way." Britt pointed two chubby thumbs at herself.

"Ugh, I wish I would have." I slid the ringer tee over my head. "But you damn southerners and your charm, it gets me every time!"

Britt laughed. I knew she wasn't thrilled about this situation at all, with her crush on Blaine and all, but she actually seemed to enjoy my new found hatred for him.

∞

On my first date with Beau he was almost an hour late, my stomach was grumbling so badly, I was afraid that he would notice. I thought that my stomach would vibrate on the leather seats of his beamer and then he would never want to talk to me again. Imagine, I thought I was the one making a bad impression and he was the one who was late.

Blaine wasn't late, in fact, he actually was early. At 5:45 the doorbell rang and Britt sprang up from my bed faster than I had ever seen that girl move. I groaned as I finished putting a rubber band in my braided pigtails. I figured low braided pigtails said school marm more than school girl.

"Libby, Blaine's here!" Britt bellowed from the living room.

"Oh, Blaine how are you?" Aunt Dee practically floated over to the door. It looked like I was the only one moving slowly.

My flip flops plopped, making that annoying 'flop flop' noise, as I slowly crept out of the bedroom and into the living room. It looked like someone was actually looking forward to this date, or was just hoping to get some.

"Hey Libby." Blaine flashed a toothy grin.

It looked like he had spent all day getting ready and not just throwing on the worst clothes he could find around the room. The first thing I noticed, which I think most girls do, was his shoes. I'd only ever seen him in very dirty work boots, but it looked like he brought out the only pair of dress shoes he had. He topped that off with khakis and an actual black button-down shirt, with the sleeves rolled up since of course since Louisiana was about a million degrees at any given time of day. You could actually see the sweat start to glisten on his arms, or maybe that was just from nervousness.

One of us was not dressed appropriately.

"Hey Blaine." I muttered, slowly making my way over to the door.

"My, Mr. Crabtree, you look so handsome! My niece is so lucky to have a guy like you taking her out!" Aunt Dee was practically drooling as she patted his shoulder, not in the drooling way like Britt, but in the 'I'm so proud this young man is taking my niece out' way. Little did she know this was the same guy that screwed half the town.

"Yeah Blaine." I looked up and met his eyes. "You clean up well." I really should stop meeting his eyes, they were bluer than the Mediterranean Sea and I couldn't stop from getting lost in them. It almost made me forget that I hated him.

"Uh, yeah." I think Blaine actually got a little red as he looked down and absently ran a hand through his hair. "You look good too Libby. But I think you can wear anything and still look amazing."

Our eyes met again, we were behaving like twelve

year olds.

Britt rolled her eyes. "Are y'all just going to stand in the doorway all night or what?"

"Uh, no." I glanced over at Brittany. "Mr. Blaine here owes me dinner."

"You are letting him take you out in that?" Aunt Dee looked me up and down with furrowed brows.

"It's comfortable. And I'm so hot and worn out from work that I didn't have the energy to change." I smiled at Aunt Dee.

"Oh, yeah, it takes a lot of energy to sit on your butt at the shop," Britt mocked. I shot her an evil glare.

"And on that note." Blaine looked back at me. "You ready?"

"Ready." I smirked at Brittany. "Bye Britt."

Then I kissed Aunt Dee on the cheek. "I shouldn't be too late."

"Oh, don't worry about it." Aunt Dee called as we headed out the door. Britt mumbled something but I couldn't understand it, probably something rude.

Blaine opened the passenger side door of his truck for me. I guess he was trying that whole southern gentleman thing.

"You know I can open my own car door," I quipped.

"Yeah, but so can I."

He hopped over on the driver's side and started the truck up as I closed the big red door behind me.

"So where did you want to go? I was thinking New Orleans is only about 45 minutes away. I could take you down to the French Quarter. Maybe stop at Café Du Monde for coffee afterwards."

It looked like Blaine was either actually trying to

impress me, or he did a lot of work to get what he wanted.

"You guys have one of those drive-in restaurants like in the movies right?"

Blaine cocked an eyebrow and glanced at me as he turned out of the driveway.

"Sam's? The drive-in?"

"Yeah." I nodded. "My sorority sisters used to love to go to the drive-ins, but the closest one was like an hour away so we would sometimes take late night road trips there. But I haven't had it in like forever, and I really could use a root beer float, served courtesy of a girl on roller skates."

Blaine laughed a deep belly laugh. "I offer to take you to the French Quarter and you would rather have Sam's?"

"Yes." I folded my arms across my chest and jutted out my bottom lip into a pout. "And you don't need to laugh at me about it."

He stopped laughing and let out a deep breath, the kind that someone takes after a long laugh. "I'm sorry Libby." He put his hand on my knee. "It's just funny that I got all dressed up, trying to impress you, and you walk out wearing flip flops and ask me to take you to Sam's." He moved one of his hands from the steering wheel and placed it on my knee.

His touch sent an immediate tingle from my legs and straight up to the area that would definitely be off limits for the night. I hated that his hand did that to me, but at the same time I almost wanted to keep it there.

"I just kind of feel like a jackass now."

I pushed his hand off my knee. It's not that I didn't

like it, I did. A lot, but I wasn't going to let him just hump and dump.

"Well you kind of are a jackass aren't you?"

"Huh?" Blaine glanced over at me as we headed down the road toward the main drag. His lower jaw actually dropped before he started talking again. "I apologized for that Libby, and you know I'm genuinely sorry. I even brought you flowers."

"I'm not talking about that. I'm over that now."

"Well then what is it?"

"Well." I bit my bottom lip and looked out the window.

"Oh come on Libby. Just tell me what's bothering you."

"Okay." I took a deep breath and looked straight out the window ahead. I didn't want to look at him as I spilled everything Dina had told me at work, and from what I had gotten out of Britt. Everything from hooking up with snaggletooth from work, to his rumored affairs with married woman, and the head count that Britt told me would rival Hugh Hefner.

We were silent for a moment, and it happened to be the moment we were pulling into Sam's. He put the car into park. He turned and just stared at me, not saying anything just staring.

I shrugged my shoulders. "Well, say something!" I put my hands out toward him like I was expecting him to hand me something.

He sighed. "I'm not going to lie to you Libby." He looked down and fiddled with his keys. "Most of that stuff people were saying is true, maybe some of it a little over-exaggerated, but true."

My nimble fingers twirled the end of one of my

braids and I bit down on my bottom lip. "Really?"

Great, I really was sitting next to Hugh Hefner.

"But." He looked back up at me and put his hand on my knee again.

"I meant it when I say that I actually do want to get to know you. I didn't take you out tonight just to sleep with you."

I looked up and met his gaze again.

"I feel really bad about your first impression of me, and I really like the fact that you aren't afraid to tell me what you think and seem to enjoy defying everything anyone else says. It's why I know, even if I tried, you probably would rather punch me than screw me."

I giggled. "It's true."

"Now let me order you your damn root beer float so I can make more of a fool of myself."

We ordered our food and instead of sitting in the truck, Blaine suggested we go to a small little grassy area a little ways away.

"You aren't taking me out to the swamp to have your way with me are you?"

Blaine cocked an eyebrow, glancing back at me, as we made our way through a few trees. "It's just a little grassy knoll. It's more comfortable to sit on than in my truck all night."

"Grassy knoll? Are we going to be shooting the president too?" I laughed, thinking that my own cleverness was rather funny.

"No Libby, we won't be shooting the president." He rolled his eyes and went back walking up what looked like just a small grass mound. "We don't really have much for hills in Louisiana, so this is what we get, knolls."

"Fine, but you will not brainwash me into shooting any presidents." I plopped down on the ground with a brown bag in one hand and my root beer float in the other.

"You are something else you know that, Libby?" He sat down beside me, resting his elbows on his knees.

"I think the term you are looking for is natural blonde." I took a sip of my root beer float and then rustled my hand through his bleach blonde hair.

It wasn't the mess of straw that it looked like and felt like a new coat sliding through my fingers. I could have kept my hand there all day, but I quickly moved them back to my lap.

"Hey my mom's a hairdresser, so she does this for me. You can blame her." He actually cracked a smile.

"Well my mom's a lawyer so you can blame her for my wit and political references." I took another long slurp.

"That explains it." Blaine unwrapped his burger and took a big bite.

"Explains what?" I stopped slurping to meet his eyes.

"I actually got nothing. I think I just like to get a rise out of you." He laughed and I shoved him a little.

The shove honestly didn't do much. Trying to move him was like trying to push a house. Part of me just wanted to actually see his biceps and feel his muscles, but I think that would have been really creepy. For a second I actually wondered what it would be like to see him completely naked, but quickly shook that off. There would be no sexing for

Blaine and Libby, not that night anyways.

"So what is with you and trying to get me all crazy anyways?" I quickly changed the subject and popped a curly fry in my mouth.

"What do you mean?" Blaine managed to get out between mouthfuls.

"I mean, you have this genuine concern for my well-being and you don't like it at all when I do anything, like, sexy and I don't understand why. I mean you don't know me, but you act like you need to protect me."

Blaine put his burger down on the bag and looked down, a somber expression on his face. "You don't know too much about your Aunt Dee's family do you?"

"No, not really. Last time Aunt Dee came up I was like in elementary school, and that was when my grandma died. So we really didn't talk about her otherwise." I actually felt kind of bad, my dad's entire heritage was in Louisiana and our family seemed to avoid it like the plague.

"Like I've always told you, your aunt is a great lady and I'm sure you know that now." I nodded as our eyes met. "I don't know what she told you about Brittany's mom."

"Not much..." I shrugged. "I know she didn't seem like a very good person and only met up with Britt to get money."

"That's not even the half of it." Blaine took a long drink out of the unmarked Styrofoam cup. "My sisters were just a few years younger than Joni and I was of course a lot younger, but I can still remember what she used to be like. I remember my sisters just admiring her. They would come home from school and talk about how Joni's hair looked that day, or ask my mom if she could do their makeup like Joni's."

After seeing Britt and Aunt Dee, I really couldn't imagine this beauty queen image that he was talking about. But I knew my father was an attractive guy, and I'm sure Aunt Dee and Britt had potential.

"Every year on the Fourth of July we have a big parade and fair. When I was about four Joni was the fair queen. Everyone watched her as she rode in the back of the mayor's convertible, at that moment I honestly thought she was the most beautiful girl anyone had ever seen."

He looked ahead with an almost distant and reminiscent look in his eyes. "I still remember she had long red hair and the whitest smile I think there ever was, but..." He looked down for what seemed like an entire minute then back up at me. "I think that was the last time she ever smiled."

"What do you mean?" I hadn't realized until that moment that I was so enthralled with what he was saying, that I was so close to him that our sides were touching, and that he had leaned his body into me. But at that point I actually found comfort in it. This wasn't the Blaine that I saw that night at the party, or Blaine the playboy, this was Blaine the new closest thing I had to a confidante in Louisiana.

He put his hand on my knee. "That night there was a big party, my sisters were too young to go and I thank God every day that they didn't go." He began rubbing my knee. "Well, at that party it seemed like a lot of guys thought Joni was the prettiest girl they had ever seen too." His voice got quite, almost angry.

"They found her the next morning in a ditch, passed out, a few miles from town. The man that found her thought she just had gotten drunk and stumbled there, but then he saw what really had happened. "

Blaine's grip tightened on my knee. "She was so beaten up and bloody, and she was completely lucid; not drunk or even drugged. That man that found her rushed her to the hospital. Two months later they found out she was pregnant, and she had no idea who the father was."

He looked back at me. "I didn't want that to happen to you. All I could think about was how good you looked at that party. Then when I saw every other guy looking at you there, I didn't want what happened to Joni to happen to you. I couldn't bear to see Dee suffer again."

He put his arm around me. "And I would never let anything like that happen to you." He leaned in, never taking his gaze off of me until his lips met mine.

CHAPTER 10

After just one date, Blaine and I had become the talk of the town. I guess it had something to do with the fact that we became inseparable.

After only a week we had seen each other just about every moment of every day that we could. He would show up at work, on my lunch break, to bring me curly fries and a root beer float from Sam's. At night he would stay at Aunt Dee's from dinner time until he couldn't take Britt glaring at us any longer and it would be way past time Aunt Dee slipped off to bed.

We would hold hands walking down the street and my phone was overloaded with pictures of the two of us. Needless to say, it was obvious that I was falling for a Louisiana boy.

"Are you going out with Blaine again tonight?" Aunt Dee asked between mouthfuls of chicken fried steak.

"I don't think they could breathe too long without each other," Britt quipped, swirling the green beans around on her plate.

I shot a glare over at Britt and then smiled back at Aunt Dee. "He's supposed to come by after dinner. I didn't want to come between a southern boy and his momma's cooking. Though he swears yours is better." I picked up a piece of steak with my fork. "But don't tell his mom that!" I laughed.

Britt rolled her eyes and Aunt Dee shared my laugh.

"Don't you have some rich boyfriend back in Illinois or something?" Britt literally spat, making a piece of gravy fly out of her mouth and across the table.

"Brittany." Aunt Dee scowled.

"No. It's fine." I turned my whole body toward Britt. Now she was just making me angry. I dealt with the glares all week and her making comments like 'Do you even know where LSU is,' when Blaine would turn on Sports Center. But now it was just getting old.

"What is your problem Britt?"

I knew the answer to that one, so before she could even open her mouth, I put up a finger as to say give me a minute.

"Look. I know you have some sort of little crush on Blaine and I'm sorry that I went on that first date with him. I honestly didn't think it would turn into anything and I honestly didn't think I'd have this strong of feelings for him."

She looked down at her plate silently. She couldn't even look me in the eye.

"I am sorry for hurting you. I truly am. You're my family and like one of my best and only friends here." I picked up the fork and put it to my lips, but paused before putting the piece of meat into my mouth. "But at the same time I do really like Blaine, and I don't want to lose you at the expense of having him as my boyfriend."

She sat silent and then slowly inched her chin up until our eyes met.

"Is he your boyfriend?"

"What?"

"You heard me." Her accent got deeper. "Is he your boyfriend?"

"Well..." I put my fork down.

"Well is he or isn't he? It's not that hard of a question." Britt pounded the table with her chubby little fist.

"Brittany, behave!" Aunt Dee remarked. The woman barely raised her voice and when she did it still didn't have much of an effect.

"No." I put my hand up toward Aunt Dee. "It's fine, I've got this." I turned my attention back toward Britt. "No, he's not my boyfriend. I mean he like hasn't asked anything official."

It wasn't like Beau did either. One day I kind of just requested him as 'in a relationship' on Facebook and he confirmed it. Unfortunately that didn't stop him from sleeping with half of the girls on campus.

"Well then how do you know he's not going off with other girls after he leaves here?" She stood up from the table. I tried to respond but she stopped me, almost screaming. "How do you know he's not just like your so-called boyfriend back home? Maybe he's just with you because you're pretty and blonde, but that's it. When he wants a real relationship he doesn't want it with some airhead, he wants substance!"

"Brittany!" Aunt Dee stood up from the table. "Now that's enough!"

"That's fine." Brittany leaned in toward me. "I'm finished anyways." She then looked up toward Aunt

Dee. "I'm going to Sarah's."

Before Aunt Dee could get a word in edgewise Brittany stormed out the front door and slammed it behind her.

Maybe she was right. Maybe Blaine was just like Beau, and maybe I was just an airheaded blonde.

∞

"Come on Libby, tell me what's wrong."

We sat outside the Tasty Freeze. Blaine had one hand on my knee, as he straddled the picnic bench, and the other one with a spoon full of ice cream. I couldn't even look at him. I just looked down at the banana split we were sharing.

"Nothing's wrong." I lied, mashing the banana with my spoon.

"Libby, I know we haven't been hanging out that long, but I know when something is wrong." He set down the spoon and ran his fingers through my hair. "If you keep sulking I may just have to go take your Aunt Dee out instead." He was trying to make a joke, but in my state I took it a little too personal.

"Or you could take one of your other many lady friends out." I continued absently swirling my spoon in the soupy ice cream.

"Libby, you know there is no one else. Hell, how would I even have time for anyone else? When we aren't together I'm working or sleeping. Sometimes I even fall asleep on your Aunt Dee's couch so we still are together while I'm sleeping."

He was right, but I couldn't shake off what Britt said. "You aren't wanting a girl that you can have a conversation with? A girl that actually knows what they are talking about on Sports Center?"

Blaine let out a single laugh. "Libby." He scooted closer toward me. "I actually like when you ask me why baseball players can make millions of dollars, but can't spend twelve dollars on a haircut."

I had to smile at that one.

"I like that when you get nervous you bite your bottom lip and twirl your hair. I like that you don't always know the right things to say, and really Libby, I just like you."

Our eyes met as I turned toward him. "Then why don't you want me to be your girlfriend?"

"What?" He kind of leaned back on the bench.

"Why haven't you asked me to be your girlfriend?" I tilted my head to the side as I waited for an answer.

"Is that what this is all about? You want to be my girlfriend?"

I nodded gently.

"What's wrong with what we've got now? Everyone knows in this town we're together."

That sounded like something Beau would say: why change things, this is just how college relationships go.

"I don't want to share you. I don't want to have to worry about you."

"Libby, you don't have to worry about me, and I don't want to be with any other girl than you. Everyone in this town knows it. Even the guys on the crew give me crap because I spend so much time with you." He stroked my cheek with the back of his hand.

"Then why not give it a title? Are you ashamed of having me as a girlfriend?" I slithered away from his hand.

"Ashamed of you?" Blaine blinked hard. "Libby you are the prettiest girl this town has ever seen. I think every time we walk outside for lunch every guy in town whispers: damn, how did a good old boy like Blaine land her." He smiled and tried to meet my eyes.

I sighed. "I just..."

"Baby." He took my chin in his hand and made our eyes meet. "I'm not like that asshole from school. I won't hurt you like he did."

I'd heard that one before too. I forced my head away from his grip and looked back down at the table.

"Fine, have it your way." Last time a guy said that to me it was Beau at Alpha Mu formal. He was mad because I wouldn't sleep with him, since it was my time of the month, and then went off and got a blow job from someone else's date behind the DJ booth. I looked over at Blaine with pleading eyes, hoping he wouldn't do that behind the Tasty Freeze dumpster.

No, he definitely didn't move from where we were. Instead he stood on top of the picnic table.

"Blaine, what are you doing?" I whispered looking up at him.

He shot a bright smile at me and winked.

"Attention people of Elsbury and Tasty Freeze guests!" Blaine cupped his hands and bellowed turning his hips and making a small circle on top of the picnic table. "This woman sitting at the table with me."

He pointed down at me, and I'm pretty sure my face was redder than the plastic picnic table.

"Is Libby Gentry and she is the most amazing girl in the entire world." By that time he had drawn quite a crowd of employees and patrons.

"We have been hanging out ever since she came here and it has been some of the best three weeks of my life." A big aw came from the crowd. "So in short."

He knelt down on the table in front of me and lifted my chin up with his hand until our eyes met. "Libby, I'd make a fool of myself for you any day and if you don't say you'll be my girlfriend, I think the whole town might just run us out of the Tasty Freeze."

That night Blaine was the one to make the Facebook relationship request first, and I gladly accepted.

CHAPTER 11

Blaine and I had officially been together almost two weeks, and so he thought it would be great to take me to his house for Sunday dinner.

"It's just a little thing we do. My sisters come in with their kids and you can, I guess, officially meet my parents, though I think this whole town knows who you are."

Those were his words. We were sitting on our usual bench downtown, eating curly fries from Sam's on our lunch. Ever since our first date we were definitely a permanent fixture in the town. This was something people either loved or hated. Girls were jealous and would glare at me, but all of Blaine's buddies seemed to just clap every time he would kiss me goodbye or even answer one of my texts. It was a little annoying.

Random people would come up to me and say things like: good for you, about time somebody locked down that Crabtree boy. And I don't even know how many random texts and facebook comments I got from my sorority sisters back home.

But there was one person that definitely was not happy with our new relationship, and that was Britt. For a long time she was the only person for me to talk to in the whole town, and I guess she felt like she had been replaced by Blaine. I think if it were any other boy than her crush to end all crushes, it would have been fine, but since it wasn't, she acted as if I committed some sort of a crime.

I thought that I would need to get a new outfit to meet Blaine's family, since unfortunately my wardrobe at Aunt Dee's was limited to work clothes and lying around the house clothes. Aunt Dee had the idea that I take Thursday off of work and take Britt with me into New Orleans. She thought I could maybe get a new bedspread and some clothes, and just spend some time with Britt. I thought it would definitely be a good chance to talk to Britt, or at least just have some fun.

"Are you sure you don't want me to go with you? I can take the afternoon off." Blaine breathed on the other line. I could tell he was trying to speak quietly so that the rest of the road crew couldn't hear him.

"Blaine, I'm a big girl, and I have Britt with me. I'm sure we will be fine in New Orleans on a Thursday afternoon." I had him on speaker phone as I slipped a t-shirt over my head. I was almost shouting into the phone.

"But what if Brittany doesn't know her way somewhere? How are you going to get around?"

I giggled. "Blaine, we're fine! We have our internet directions and if we get lost we'll just stop and ask for directions."

Blaine groaned.

"And besides, I need some girl time and shopping time. If you were allowed in my bedroom you would see that I have a bubblegum pink bedspread that badly needs to be replaced." I checked myself out in the mirror and put the phone back up to my ear, taking it off of speaker. "Besides, if you take off of work you will lose valuable money that could be used to get us more root beer floats."

I could hear him smiling on the other end. He did this cute little thing where he would blow air out of his nose when he smiled. "Alright Libby, well text me when you get home alright?"

"Alright, now get back to work."

I heard my bedroom door creak open just as I hung up the phone.

"You know if you'd rather go with Blaine than me, I understand." Britt was standing in the doorway swaying back and forth.

"Of course I want to go with you. I think Blaine and I spend enough time together, and I could definitely use some girl time." I plopped my phone in my purse and cracked a big toothy grin at Britt.

"Well I'm not much for shopping." Britt shifted back and forth on her flip flop clad feet.

"Well I think we can change that. Now come on." I stomped on over to her and looped my arm through hers. "I don't think the Grand Am goes over fifty, and I'd really like to get there before I'm thirty." It was the first time in a long time Britt actually cracked a smile.

∞

The whole car ride was almost silent except for the country songs that blared on the radio. Britt still seemed to be mad at me, but I was going to have a good shopping day no matter what. It was my first time in New Orleans and I just really wanted to see everything.

The French Quarter was every bit as beautiful as I imagined. I loved looking up at every single iron terrace and even getting my heels caught in the cobblestone street. I thought maybe I should have let Blaine take me there on our first date, but maybe he would have been as bored with me as Britt was. She seemed to yawn about every five seconds and would just roll her eyes every time I would squeal at a building I had seen in a movie.

"I think we've seen enough places Brad Pitt may have touched during Interview with the Vampire, can we go find whatever you need and go?" Britt sulked, crossing her arms across her chest.

"Fine." I almost skipped toward a boutique as Brittany dawdled behind me.

"But this is going to be fun!" I thought maybe if I just stayed positive then maybe Britt would too. A shop keeper nodded in our direction, but was busy showing a blue-haired lady a very expensive looking watch.

"So." Britt glanced at me from behind a rack of dresses. "Do you really like Blaine..?"

I held up a pale yellow sundress in front of me. I was definitely not sure if I could still fit in a size six, and I was beginning to wonder how this was going to work out for Kristi's wedding.

I was also not looking forward to having this conversation with Britt. She always gave me second thoughts about Blaine whenever we would talk. Sometimes it would turn into something good, and sometimes it would just cause an argument.

"Well, yeah, I mean he is my boyfriend." I grabbed

another dress off of the rack to keep my hands busy.

She looked down and shifted from one foot to the other. "I just don't understand how you knew I liked him, and then met him." She looked up and put her hands outward toward me. "Then you absolutely hated him, then after one night y'all are inseparable, and I have to just sit and watch you cuddle on MY couch with my crush to end all crushes."

I put the dress down and just looked at Brittany for a moment. What could I say? Would anything really make it better? I didn't want to just humor her and say there were plenty of other guys out there, and it would just be mocking for me to say she was too young for him anyways.

"You know." I sighed. "Before college not even a single guy looked at me."

Brittany rolled her eyes. "Oh please, like I haven't heard that ugly duckling story a million times before." She twirled her hair and in a mocking high voice uttered, "don't worry Brittany, once you fill out you'll be gorgeous. You know when I was younger I got picked on all the time and I turned out okay."

She stopped with the mocking voice and twirling her hair. Then she looked straight at me with a determined look on her face. "People can say that it gets better all they want, but when you're living in the now, and you see every other girl in your class get a date, every other girl in your class even get looked at by a boy, and you get nothing but horrible nicknames and terrible stories to come home and cry about."

I could see the tears almost welling up in her eyes, but she pushed them back.

Then I thought about Brittany's mom. The beauty

queen whose reign ended the night Brittany was conceived. I winced when I realized that it wasn't all about me this time. Brittany never would be the beauty queen that her mother was and would always be haunted with the memory of what became of her.

"You know what?" I walked over to her and put my arm around her. She was so short her head was practically at my chest. "This place is a bit out of my price range anyways. You want to get out of here? Maybe I'll take you to the batting cages?"

Britt actually looked up at me and smiled. "Really?"

"Sure. I'm not used to usually having a budget, but I'm sure we could find me a dress and a bedspread at Wal-Mart or something."

"So what about you and your boyfriend back at school anyways?" Brittany piped up as we walked toward the car. "I know you told me he cheated on you and stuff, but what does he think about you and Blaine? If I don't like it he must really not like it."

I sighed. The last thing I wanted to talk about was Beau, and I could just imagine what he was saying about me to all of his fraternity brothers. "Remember how I told you that guys didn't even look at me in high school?"

"Psh, yeah and you act like I really believe that one." Brittany opened her car door and I slid in after she did. "You're blonde, tall, and skinny and you think I believe you didn't have guys begging for your number like they are here?"

"Well." I started the car. "See here's the thing. In a big high school, people don't even notice who you are if you're not popular. And with blonde wavy hair and being as tall as I am, I got the nickname Big Bird in middle school that just kind of stuck with me."

Brittany laughed. "You? Big Bird?"

"It's completely true! Boys used to ask me how to get to Sesame Street and girls would constantly ask if Elmo and I had the same hairstylist."

"You definitely aren't getting picked on and called Big Bird now. You're like a sorority princess." Britt pointed out as I pulled out of the parking spot.

I took a deep breath. "Yes, I may have learned a thing or two about using a diffuser, and I may have joined a sorority, but honestly none of that would have ever happened if I didn't start dating Beau."

"Huh?" Brittany turned down the radio and looked straight at me. I caught her out of the corner of my eye, and her own eyes were filled with bewilderment. "What do you mean if it wasn't for Beau?"

"Since I was so painfully shy in high school, and since my mom and sister were in sororities in college, they thought I should rush. Of course the only reason any sorority even looked at me was because my mom and sisters were legacies." I took a deep breath.

"And then along came Beau. He was treasurer of Alpha Mu, one of the biggest fraternities on campus, and after meeting me at a party he immediately dubbed me Legs. He decided that my long legs and blonde hair where something that was actually desirable, instead of something that belongs on PBS."

A stray strand of hair poked in front of my face and I pushed it back.

"So basically if I hadn't met Beau I would still be Big Bird, and instead of being the sorority ditz I would have just been another dumb blonde girl."

"Wow." Britt breathed. "You actually are human

after all."

I laughed. It was the first time all day that I think I had.

"Well, I guess I am if you say so. I guess I am just another broke human."

"So, do you think Blaine is going to be anything like Beau?" God she was full of questions.

"What do you mean?" I glanced at my blind spot before switching lanes then glancing back at Britt.

"He kind of has that player reputation and so did Beau. Aren't you worried about that?"

It was actually something I was very worried about. I didn't want to get hurt again like I was with Beau, and even though Blaine assured me over and over again that he was nothing like Beau and his playboy days were over, it was still always in the back of my mind.

"No...I mean yes...I mean." I took a deep long sigh. "I mean I really don't know. I'm always worried about it no matter how many times he tells me he's over that."

"Are you doing him?"

"BRITTANY!"

"Well it's an honest question." She laughed.

"What's with all the questions anyways?" I spotted the exit for Elsbury up ahead and veered over into the right lane.

"I just want to know. I mean we haven't really talked lately, and you know, just catching up."

"Well if you really must know. No, no we haven't slept together."

She leaned in closer. "Does that worry you?"

I shook my head and tilted it to the side. "Why

would that worry me?"

"Do you think he could be getting it somewhere else? Or maybe he doesn't find you attractive or something?" Britt rattled off.

"So I tell you that I get called Big Bird in high school and you go and tell me that my boyfriend won't sleep with me because he's cheating on me and thinks that I am ugly?" I was visibly upset now. My hands tightened on the steering wheel as I started speaking through clenched teeth.

Maybe Britt was right. Maybe Blaine just wanted to get with the most interesting new thing in town and would dump me once I got old. I had hoped it wouldn't take me that long to figure it out.

CHAPTER 12

"Libby, you got mail!" Britt shouted from the living room.

It had been two days since we went to New Orleans, and I couldn't get what Britt had said out of my head. I had avoided even seeing Blaine. It had been three days without seeing each other and I was wondering if by now he had found someone new.

He would come to the office with lunch and I would tell him that I was too busy, or he would want to come over to Aunt Dee's after work and I would make up some excuse. I promised him I would still go over there for Sunday dinner and maybe then he would break up with me, or just keep me around as a trophy girlfriend.

I put the last of the pillows on my new bedspread (black and red, no more bubblegum pink), and walked out to the living room. Brittany handed me a big white envelope with my name scribbled out in a fancy writing on the front. I opened it up to find another envelope reading 'Libby and guest.' It was Kristi's wedding invitation.

"Guess what I got in the mail?" I teased, dialing Kristi as soon as I opened the invitation.

"Oh Em Gee, you finally got it! I was started to think I had the wrong address!" Kristi squealed on the other end, for someone getting married she still talked like a teenage girl.

"Yep, I couldn't let you be down a bridesmaid." I smiled. Britt rolled her eyes at me as she grabbed a cookie from the jar in the kitchen.

"And are you bringing Mr. Louisiana with you? I think I have to approve of my little sister's new boyfriend!"

I didn't even think about asking Blaine, okay the thought had crossed my mind a few times, but would he really want to go? Even if he did what would he think of me with all my friends? A bunch of Chicago girls in designer dresses talking about shoes and makeup? I was sure that he would love that. He'd probably love to meet Beau even more. I could just imagine how that one would go over.

"I'll be sure to ask him." I beamed.

What could it hurt? If he really did want to be with me, not Big Bird, not Legs, but Libby, then he would have to go to this wedding.

"Well you know Beau has been asking a lot about you ever since you made it Facebook official with Mr. Louisiana." Kristi added.

"Really? I honestly didn't think he would care. He was the one who cheated on me and broke it off." I honestly couldn't imagine Beau caring in the slightest. At first I wondered if Kristi had made it up, but then remembered her fiancé, Gabe, and Beau were frat brothers so they probably had talked about it.

"It came up between him and Gabe one night."

That didn't really give me much to go off of, so I pressed for more.

"What did he say exactly?" I pushed.

"Like, okay. We were hanging out at the lake and he was all, 'well it's kind of skanky or whatever for her to move on so quickly'. And I was just like whatever." You could hear Kristi chomping on her gum as she talked. It really made her seem like a teenager between all the chomping.

"Well he doesn't have any reason to be upset. He is the one that broke it off with me," I quipped.

"I don't know. He's probably just jealous or whatever. But hey sweetie I gotta go! Say hi to Mr. Louisiana for me!" She hung up before I could even get a goodbye in, which was actually alright because my mom quickly buzzed in.

"Hey Mom."

That was a surprise. It was the first time that I had heard from her since I'd gotten to Louisiana. Well except for a few e-mails.

"Okay, listen."

"Hello and how are you, to you too."

I heard my mom groan. "Libby I don't have much time and this is important."

"Okay let's hear it."

"So I got off of the phone with your advisor and he just informed me that you can file for an appeal to get back into school for the fall." My mother, the non-stop lawyer.

"Well wouldn't that take a lot of work?" I twirled a strand of hair.

"Libby, if you had put a lot of work into your schooling in the first place we wouldn't have this problem. Don't you want to go back to school?"

It was something that was constantly on my mind. I knew I wouldn't have much of a future if I didn't go back and I knew it was what was best for me. I also never thought that I would actually be starting to enjoy Louisiana. On the other hand it wasn't like Blaine was really giving me much of a reason to stay, and it would make Beau even more pissed off if I came back.

"Alright Mom, what do I have to do?"

CHAPTER 13

I was never nervous on our first date, but I was sure as hell nervous to meet Blaine's family. I never actually met Beau's family, even on family weekend. He said I didn't have to, that it was too much of an inconvenience. Even though he met mine right away. I should have really listened to my sister when she said he was nothing more than a juiced-up dirt bag.

"Can you zip me up?" I turned my back toward Britt.

I decided to go with a sleeveless, violet baby doll dress. It wasn't anything too fancy since I definitely couldn't afford that. I also thought it looked okay to meet Blaine's parents.

"Yeah, I guess." Her chubby little fingers struggled with the zipper as she slowly fastened the dress. Clearly I needed to do something before Kristi's wedding. I never gained weight in school and as Kristi told me earlier in the week, I may have to start praying to the porcelain god if I wanted the bridesmaid dress to fit.

"Do I look alright?" I did a little twirl, holding my arms above my head.

"Yeah, you do Libby, you really do." Britt couldn't look me in the eye. She just stared down at her feet.

"Look Libby, I'm sorry for what I said about you

and Blaine. I was really jealous, and well I thought if I started making you second guess your relationship. I don't know." She stopped and shifted her weight again. "I do think he really does like you Libby, and I'm sorry. I really am."

I smiled and leaned down to kiss Britt's forehead. She cocked an eyebrow in response.

"Britt, you're fine. I can understand how you felt and no matter what, you're my favorite little cousin."

This girl needed some kind of a role model in her life. I knew Aunt Dee could do all the motherly stuff, while I could do the girly things.

"So, you're not going to break up with Blaine and he'll start coming over again?"

I cocked my head to the side. "You want Blaine to start coming over again? So you can watch us cuddle on the couch and watch Sports Center?"

"Well, if I can't have him I at least need something good to look at!"

We shared a laugh, an actual hard laugh.

"Girls?" Aunt Dee knocked on my door frame and interrupted our laughter.

I took a deep breath in trying to stop my laughter. "Yeah Aunt Dee?"

She moved to the side and Blaine stepped out from the living room. There I was on the floor of my bedroom, holding my stomach from laughing with Britt lying down in front of me. Of course as soon as we saw Blaine we both quickly stood up.

"Hey Blaine." I smoothed out my dress.

"So this is what you do in the bedroom." He leaned his arm above his head on the door frame, and then tilted his whole body against it. "No wonder I'm not allowed in here."

"Sorry, I thought you heard him." Aunt Dee was wringing her hands together, like she was trying to squeeze water out of them that would never come.

"It's fine Aunt Dee." I smoothed the wrinkles out of my skirt and hopped over to Blaine. "So are you just going to make fun of me all night or are you taking me over to your parents?"

∞

Blaine's parent's house was only a few miles from Aunt Dee's, and even more off of the beaten path than I thought was possible. But his house was definitely like something out of a magazine.

It was a cute, little, white Plantation style home, but definitely smaller. Like a Cape Cod with a big front porch, complete with a wooden porch swing. It wasn't anything like a grand Antebellum home that you would see in the movies, but it definitely had character. He pulled his truck over to the side of the house and turned off the engine.

"Do you think they're actually going to like me?" I bit my lip, twirling my thumbs in my hand.

"Do you think you're going to stop ignoring me like you have been?"

I abruptly turned my head toward him. "What?"

"Libby, you've been ignoring me for days now, with the lamest excuses. Headaches, Jeopardy, and I just want to know what's going on." He cupped my face in his hands and pulled me closer to him.

"If you are going to break up with me, please just tell me now, so I don't have to introduce you to my parents. Then have my crazy sister, Meg, try and put a curse on you or something."

I giggled, but he looked at me with eyes of steel. "I'm serious, Libby."

"Well, are you breaking up with me?" I cocked my head, as much as I could with it being in his hands.

"What? Libby why would you even think that?" He put his hands down and unbuckled his seatbelt. "You know I'm crazy about you."

"Yeah, but how many other girls have you told that to? I mean, UGH." I slumped down in my seat and put my head in my hands. "I don't know what to think! I think I probably think too much."

"Libby." He pulled me, by the waist, close to him and slanted my chin up toward him. "Look, I care about you, and just stop thinking about your ex. I'm not like him. The past is all you have with him, and the past is the past the future is now."

I grinned. "Did you just quote Christopher Walken?"

"Yes. Yes I did. Does it do anything for you?" He pressed his forehead against mine.

"Oh yeah." I leaned in and kissed him lightly on the lips, and then he pulled me closer into a full blown tongue-in-cheek kiss.

But before we could get too into it I heard a rap on the window. I jumped almost across the seat after looking out to see a little pigtailed girl staring back at me.

"Uncle Blaine's eatin' da blonde lady!" The little girl squealed. A pair of bronzed arms pulled her off of the hood of the truck.

Blaine threw open the truck and grabbed the

pigtailed girl. "Abby Cadabby!" he screamed, throwing her up in the air as she squealed.

"We were wondering where y'all was at!" The bronzed woman said. She threw her arms around Blaine and the little girl.

"You may be sittin' outside suckin face with your girlfriend, but that ain't gonna stop you from giving your sister a hug." She had one of the thickest southern accents that I had ever heard. I felt like that was my cue to get out of the truck. I slowly opened the door and saw a freckle-faced little boy staring up at me.

"Um...hi..." I waved down at the little boy.

His response was just to shriek loudly. Blaine and his sister ran over with the little girl in tow. Blaine's sister knelt down in front of the little boy.

"Shh, Braiden it's okay." She ran her hands through his hair and stroked his cheek. Her bright blonde hair fell in a mess all over her face as she wiped the boy's runny nose.

"What'd you do to him, Libby?" Blaine nudged my elbow, the little girl was still in his arms.

"I didn't do anything." My face heated up. I bit my bottom lip, unsure of what to do next.

"Oh, I'm kidding with you, Libby." Blaine put an arm around me and kissed my forehead.

"Ew, gross Uncle Blaine!" The little girl shrieked. I realized she was in a big pink tutu and had a sparkly purple tiara on top of those brown pigtails.

"Libby, meet my niece Abby." He held the little girl up in the air as she giggled. "And the little boy that you scared is Braiden. And this is my sister Meg," he exclaimed as Meg picked up Braiden and stood up, looking me up and down.

"So you're the girl that finally nailed down my brother." She had an aura about her that could scare the crap out of you. I knew she could probably toss me around without me having known what hit me.

"Um." I looked over at Blaine for some back up and he just shrugged. I looked back at Meg. "I guess."

She threw her arms around me and embraced me in a big hug, all the while Braiden was still in one arm.

When she let go she just looked at me. "Any girl who could rope my brother in a relationship is a good girl in my book."

I smiled weakly as she let go of me.

"Now come on, let's get you two in the house so you can meet the rest of the zoo." That syrupy thick accent flew out of Meg's lips.

I grabbed a pie that Aunt Dee had made and carried it in the house with us. I firmly believed that no matter where you were going, if you were invited over to someone's house you should always bring something. And since my mom was an attorney, she didn't cook, it was usually wine or catered by the grocery store bakery. But I thought it would be better if Aunt Dee made one of her pecan pies than me bringing something from the grocery store.

A short stocky woman in an apron with bright blonde hair (what was with these Crabtrees and their hair?) stepped out onto the porch as we approached it.

"Grandma!" Abby squealed as she jumped out of Blaine's arms. She ran up to the lady and pulled on the bottom of her shorts. "We found Blaine. He was eatin dat girl's face in his twuck!" Abby exclaimed proudly.

"Is that so?" The woman cooed in a thick southern accent. She looked down at Abby then at Blaine and me. "So, this is why we were waiting on you for dinner!"

I bit my bottom lip as Blaine put an arm around me, edging me toward the front porch. "Ma, this is my girlfriend Libby, and Libby this is my mom, Vicki."

I thrusted the pie out toward Vicki, not even looking up and blurted, "My Aunt Dee made pie."

Meg and Vicki shared a loud laugh. It was almost melodious with their thick country accents.

"Why, aren't you just a peach?" Vicki exclaimed as she took the pie. "Your Aunt Dee makes the best pecan pie in three Parishes."

I nodded, looking up at Blaine for reassurance. He kissed my forehead and looked down at me.

"Come on, let's get inside."

We entered into a small foyer with a little fireplace directly in front of us and a large picture of the family, from when Blaine had to be about ten, stood directly facing me. Off to the side I could hear men screaming. They were around a TV that couldn't have been more than 30 inches, and the three men were crowded around it sitting on worn out floral print couches.

"Boys!" Vicki shouted with determination.

"Oh man is that the LSU game?" Blaine peered over my shoulder.

"Yeah, they're going into extra innings!" A younger looking man with a trucker cap and a five o'clock shadow glanced over at us, then went straight back to looking at the TV. I figured he must have been Braiden's dad the way that Braiden ran over to him.

I was starting to think this time I was the one that was overdressed. Besides Abby's tutu, everyone else was in shorts and t-shirts. I wanted to make a good impression, but this time I was starting to feel a little self-conscious.

"Arthur." Vicki bellowed.

"What is it, Vicki?" A man looking to be about in his mid-forties with thick brown curly hair, that held specks of gray, and a Colonel Mustard mustache looked over at us. He was about to turn back toward the TV, but then he got up when he realized I was standing there.

"Oh, pardon me." He stood up and slowly walked over to us. He had a voice that sounded almost like John Wayne. "I'm Blaine's dad, Arthur." He extended his hand out to me and I shook it weakly.

The man with the trucker hat came darting behind Blaine's dad, and a shorter tanned guy with jet-black hair and a baby face came in flying behind him.

"Damn Blaine, looks like you done alright," The Jet black haired guy exclaimed.

"Hush up Ronnie." A very pregnant woman with long, stringy blonde hair came down the small hallway, waddling toward us. She smacked the guy upside the head with her free hand since she was carrying a sniffling toddler in the other, and then turned back toward me. "Don't listen to him. He's just mad cuz he ain't getting none till after the baby's born."

"Really Alicia?" Blaine shook his head. "And in front of Marcus too?"

Alicia shrugged and the boys returned to huddle around the TV.

"Well, dinner will just be a little while longer. Why don't you show Libby around and I'll call y'all when we're ready?" Blaine's mom interrupted. I was just happy to be getting out of the foyer for a little bit. It was definitely a lot to take in.

We saw the red and white kitchen that carried fresh smells of Andouille gumbo, shrimp creole, and pralines. My mouth watered as we continued out to the little back porch, that housed two huge Bloodhounds who happily barked as we passed, and then through the dining room. Pictures of the kids and grandkids surrounded the house, that really could use a few coats of paint in most of the rooms, but you could tell that it was filled with love.

My parents' house was pristinely decorated and had more than enough coats of paint, but I honestly couldn't even say if there was a single picture of my sister and I anywhere around the house.

We went down the hall to see two bedrooms and a bathroom. I guess there was another bathroom in his parents' bedroom over on the other side of the house, but I really couldn't imagine three kids sharing one bathroom. Hardwood floors creaked throughout the house, but I was starting to fall in love with its old charm. The next area Blaine was really excited to take me to was, of course, his bedroom.

Blaine and his dad had refinished the attic a couple years ago, he told me, and it was a pretty big space that was surrounded by wooden planks and a pretty low ceiling. Blaine and I really had to crouch in some areas. A very large bed sat underneath a small window and right next to it on the night stand was a picture. It was a really horrible picture of the two of us. It was us lying on what had been dubbed 'our grassy knoll'. I was laughing in the picture and Blaine was kissing my forehead. I recognized it as his Facebook picture as well.

"Really Blaine?" I picked up the picture, as he leaned against the dresser across from his bed. "Out of all the pictures we have from my phone and that I put on Facebook, and you picked this one?"

He shrugged. "I like that one."

I rolled my eyes. "Fine." Then something caught my eye, off in the corner by his closet I spotted an acoustic guitar. I walked over to it and picked it up, looking back up at Blaine.

"Do you actually play?"

He slowly walked over to me. "Of course I play. Did you think I just keep it around for decoration?"

"How about you play me something then?" He wasn't much taller than me, maybe about a couple of inches, but I always felt like I was looking up at him.

"Well." He took the guitar out of my hand and then slung it around himself. "Then I'd have to take it from you."

"I don't mind." I plopped down on the bed.

"Well what do you want to hear?" He gradually walked over and sat down next to me.

"Surprise me." I leaned back so that I was propped up on my elbows.

He took a pick out of his pocket and started slowly strumming the guitar, and then he started playing something familiar. He strummed the first familiar chords to Brown Eyed Girl. He looked up from the guitar and smiled at me, leaning in closer.

He looked over at me as he sang the last brown eyed girl part. He sounded like a mixture of Billy Ray Cyrus and John Mayer, a kind of indie-country rock. I have to admit it was pretty hot. Then he leaned and whispered in a half sing-songy voice.

"You are my brown eyed girl."

I smiled and wrinkled my nose as he leaned in and kissed me.

As I opened my mouth slightly he stopped me.

"Hold on."

I pouted out my bottom lip, so was he getting it elsewhere?

"I have to put my guitar down." He smiled blowing the air out of his nose like he always did when he smiled, and set the guitar on the ground next to the bed.

I leaned back as we began kissing again. While our mouths were busy, my hands traced down to his belt. I pulled the straps out through the loops, tracing my fingers along his underwear line. He only let me do that for about five seconds before he moved my hands back up to his shoulders. I quickly moved them back down and began fiddling with his belt again.

He pulled away and sat up.

"What's wrong?" I sat up and rested my head on his shoulder while rubbing his thigh with one hand. He obviously wasn't turned off the way his bulge pressed against his pants.

He turned his head to the side. "I just don't think we should be doing this, especially not with my parents right downstairs."

"Ugh!" I fell back on the bed. It was like I was being

enveloped in a sea of flannel sheets.

"I don't think we are ever going to do anything!" I put my hands over my eyes. "You know for being this big playboy that everyone talked about, you sure are acting like Hugh Hefner without any Viagra."

Blaine crawled up next to me, hovering over me, and then he uncovered my eyes. "Libby, I couldn't be more attracted to you."

"Then why haven't you even tried anything more than making out with me?" I pouted.

"Libby." He crouched in closer and kissed my neck and down my collar bone. "You're not like other girls I've dated. I want more than just to screw you." He slid down my body and onto the floor in front of me. "And believe me I do want to do that, BAD."

"Then why haven't you?" I cocked an eyebrow and looked down at him.

Blaine lifted up my skirt and traced his fingers up and down my thighs. "Well." He gently kissed my inner thighs, right near my knee caps. His feather-like kisses made my pulse rise and my whole body shivered underneath him. "It's not like we've had much alone time."

It was true. The more I thought about it the only time we had alone time was when we were at the grassy knoll, and I don't think I wanted to have sex on the grass. Otherwise we were in the living room at my Aunt Dee's or one of the many highly public areas in Elsbury.

"So." I pleaded, innocently batting my eyes. "You don't have another girl on the side?"

"Libby, baby, I don't think I ever could have another girl besides you."

I leaned down to the edge of the bed to kiss him, my legs completely spread and his neck strained up to me. But before I could even reach my lips to his I heard creaking on the stairs.

"Shit it's your mom!" I pushed him down on the floor, not realizing that he had a hold of me and we both went tumbling down onto the hard wooden floor.

That was the second time that night someone walked in on me, on the floor and in a dress, laughing my ass off.

Alicia stood in the door way, Marcus on one hip and a hand on the other. A confused look popped across her puffy face. "You know I thought when I'd come up here to get you for dinner, I may have found you in a different position. Not on the floor laughing."

That made us laugh even harder. I was holding my stomach as Blaine helped me up off the floor.

"Come on, dinner's ready and Blaine." She moved closer to us and messed up Blaine's hair. "You should probably fix your hair so Ma doesn't think you two were doing something else up here."

Blaine just gave a goofy grin as we followed his sister and Marcus down the stairs, with our messy hair and all.

∞

So a comparison of dinner in the Gentry house compared to dinner at the Crabtree house: When the Gentrys' have dinner, it usually involves Stouffers lasagna that's still half frozen. Complete with a bottle of scotch, courtesy of my dad. There are no prayers said before dinner and the whole family is just the three of us, sitting around a large oak dining room table with a pristine table cloth and freshly upholstered chairs. Dinner conversation usually is focused around what color to paint the kitchen for the thirtieth time or where to vacation.

Dinner at the Crabtree's' is a whole other story.

By the time we got downstairs Abby was already crying in her booster seat, which in turn made Ashley, Meg's youngest child, and Braiden cry. Then as soon as we walked in Marcus joined in on the crying.

The dining room table had been through everything from Blaine trying to saw off its legs in grade school to Alicia thinking it would be great to paint it with blue nail polish. The chairs were all missmatched and everyone gathered around the table, talking about every different conversation you can imagine. But when Blaine's dad stood up everyone was quiet and prayers were said.

"Dear Lord, we thank you for blessing us with this wonderful food and for the many gifts you have given us. From our wonderful family and the blessing of Meg and Billy and their new home."

I later found out that Meg and Billy's house was severely damaged during the last hurricane, and they had been living with Blaine's parents since it happened. Somehow they had three kids in that time, but had recently just bought a small house outside of town.

"We pray to you Lord that Alicia and Ronnie have a healthy baby to add to our beautiful family of grandchildren." All the grandkids looked up and smiled at that one. "And we thank you Lord to have

Blaine finally find a girl that he cared about enough to share his joys with and to bless us with her presence. Amen."

"Amen." Everyone said in unison. Then it was back to the chaos of dinner; kids screaming, the guys yelling across the table at each other about the baseball game, and Alicia telling me every detail about her pregnancy, which I really didn't need to know.

After dinner and pecan pie, the boys retreated to the living room, the kids in the back yard, and I offered to help with the clean up.

"So you know my baby brother hasn't brought a girl home in a long time." Meg stated as we picked up the dirty plates from the table.

"Really?" I asked, trying to be polite, I really didn't want to hear about Blaine's exes just like he really didn't want to hear about Beau.

"We all know this past year he had been kind of a tomcat. We honestly didn't know when he was going to grow out of that."

I nodded, stacking the plates on top of each other. I didn't want to hear about Blaine's sex life, especially not from his sister.

"The truth is." She sighed. "We honestly thought he'd never get over Julie."

That was the first time I had ever heard anything about a serious girlfriend Blaine had. I only knew about the many numerous girls he had been with this past year.

"Julie and him, man they were together since grade school. We all thought they'd get married someday. But then he and Julie graduated high school, and Julie got a scholarship to Ole Miss, about eight hours away."

I nodded. I really wasn't too interested at that moment.

"That's when everything changed. Blaine didn't have plans to go to college...well you know at least not right away. But he promised to go up and see her every weekend. After her first week at college, she called Blaine up and told him not to come up for the weekend." She stacked some more plates never looking up.

"Blaine was pretty upset, but thought maybe she just had some studying to do. Next weekend came and the same thing. Finally the following weekend he just drove up there. And Julie, well Julie wasn't the same little Louisiana girl we all knew. She went and joined one of them sororities you know?"

Uh oh, I didn't like where this was going. I bit my bottom lip and nodded, not looking up.

"And well, when Blaine came to visit, she had decided that she couldn't be with a boy that wasn't educated and that there was no future for them. She basically called him down home white trash and said Elsbury was her past." I could see the anger in Meg's hands, they were almost shaking as she knotted them into little fists.

"She never came back you know? Don't think she could show her face in this town again after everyone got word of what she had said. Her parents even moved out, her daddy got some kind of job transfer, or so they say."

She shook her head and clanked some silverware together, almost throwing it on top of the stacks of plates. "I never thought Blaine would get out of his slump. He would go to work and then come home almost every night for a whole month. Doing nothing but working, sleeping, and eating. Then Mama made him get out some, so he went with some of the crew to a few parties. Soon my brother was the talk of the town again. I guess he felt like if he couldn't have Julie he'd have every other girl in town."

Meg stopped stacking and looked directly at me. I tried not to meet her gaze, and it was the same steel blue as Blaine's when he was angry. "I was so worried about my brother, and I really don't want to see that happen to him again."

I nodded, trying to look down.

"I mean it." She pointed a Lee Press-On nail finger at me. "I do not want to see or hear about my brother getting hurt again. I've heard your story Libby. You may have won my parents and my husband over, but hell or high water will any girl ever hurt my brother again. Ya hear me?"

I bit my lip so hard it actually started to bleed as I was nodding furiously. I started to wonder if the only reason Blaine was with me was as a revenge tactic for his ex, but I was almost too scared to bring it up to him. I saw Meg's arms and I definitely knew that woman could do some damage.

∞

Blaine drove me home quite a bit later after my run-in with Meg. I tried to avoid making eye contact with her all night. I was afraid she had learned some voodoo and was going to be poking pins in a doll of me all night.

"Is something wrong, baby?" Blaine reached over the seat and put his arm around me. "You've been really quiet ever since dinner.

I shook my head as I looked down at floor of Blaine's truck.

Blaine sighed. "Meg told you about Julie didn't she?"

"How did you know that?" I turned sharply toward him, well as sharply as I could down a bumpy gravel road.

"I figured the way you were avoiding her after dinner something happened. That was my best guess as to something she would say. My sisters are a little over protective."

A little, I thought, maybe if a little was shanking someone in the bathroom.

"I think she thinks because I'm in a sorority that I am just like her." I spoke barely above a whisper.

"Well I do like sorority girls. Ever since I first saw a Hustler in middle school." He smiled teasingly.

I pinched his side and he laughed through a wince.

"I'm serious Blaine. I'm not going to ever do that to you. When I go back up north I'm not going to be like that. You can come and visit whenever you like. I'll even try and bake for you!" I scooted closer to him, trying to get my point across.

He slowly moved his arm out from under me and put his hand back on the wheel, saying nothing.

"What? Did I say something wrong?" I groaned. "Look, I know I suck at baking, but I can learn!"

"No, Libby. It's not that." He shook his head. "I just was hoping you really weren't planning on moving back to Chicago."

"Well it's actually the suburbs."

"Same thing!" He pulled into Aunt Dee's lot, sitting at the end of the driveway as he turned his lights off and put the car in park.

"Look Libby." He turned toward me.

"If we're going to do this I want this to be real. I don't want just some summer fling, to be that guy that passes the time for you till you get back to your shopping malls and sorority houses." He grabbed my hands and dipped his forehead down into them. "I really don't want to go through that again, and I think your Aunt Dee and Brittany really like you here too."

"Blaine, I don't know what you want me to say. That I'll stay with you in Elsbury forever? That I will never go back to school?" I moved my hands to my lap. "I really can't do that Blaine."

He sighed and put his head in his own hands.

"But." I moved my hands toward him and lifted his face into my palms. "To prove that I do want you involved in my life in and out of Louisiana, I want you to come with me to my big sister, Kristi's wedding in August. I'm one of her bridesmaids so I really have to go, but you'll get to see me in a really cute dress. I mean we'd have to get you a plane ticket for Chicago, but I'd really like you to go. I'm not ashamed to have you as my boyfriend. And if you needed to punch Beau in the face, I'd be okay with that to."

I grinned as wide as I could, hoping that would make him feel better.

He took a deep breath. "Well that all depends Libby."

I tilted my head to the side. "Depends on what?"

He leaned in, moving a hand under my dress and sliding it up to my inner thigh. His face had moved to be less than an inch from mine. "How good do you look in that bridesmaid dress?"

CHAPTER 14

I was really tired of most of Blaine and I's dates being us either going to Sam's, or sitting around Aunt Dee's, so I told him he had to take me out somewhere. Part of that was I was also hoping to get some alone time. We still hadn't had sex, and I was really wondering if we were ever going to.

I decided I better at least look somewhat attractive. After less than a month I had reverted to just wearing shorts and t-shirts around Blaine when I wasn't in work clothes. I thought that might have something to do with him not wanting to sleep with me.

I took a long shower, tried to straighten my hair, but with the humidity it was doing no such thing. I took so long getting ready in the bathroom that Britt was pounding on the door for almost five minutes straight telling me she really had to poop.

When Blaine finally came to pick me up, around seven, his eyes looked like they were going to pop out of their sockets. I tried to hold his gaze as he eyed me from the bottom of my black stilettos, up my low rise jeans, to my black satin halter top. Needless to say, if something didn't happen tonight it was definitely a waste of a cute outfit.

But I guess Blaine didn't get the memo about looking sexy. He was in his usual attire, a black shirt with a fleur-de-lis emblem, cargo shorts, and tennis shoes. I guessed we weren't going anywhere too fancy. I waved goodbye to Aunt Dee and Britt, slung my purse over my shoulder, and headed out to Blaine's truck.

"Damn, is all I've got to say," Blaine whispered, before closing his door behind him in the truck.

"I take it you like my outfit." I smirked, stretching my shoulders back in an attempt to stick out my barely-there-chest a bit more.

He made a Scooby-doo voice, shaking his face as he did so. It was like something out of a cartoon, I couldn't help but laugh.

"So where are we going tonight anyways?" I traced my fingers on the back of his earlobe when he started down the gravel path from Aunt Dee's house.

"Well a couple of my buddies wanted us to meet them at this pool hall outside of town," Blaine replied meekly.

"And you told them no, right?" I kissed his favorite spot, right where his neck meets his shoulders.

"Well..."

I pulled away and just stared at him, narrowing my eyes. "Okay, let me ask again. You did tell them no, riiiiight?"

He groaned. "Libby baby, they really wanted to meet you. I promise after a couple games of pool you and I can just go somewhere alone. Okay? I promise baby." He reached his arm out to put around me and I brushed it off.

"You owe me big sir! I don't wear these stilettos just for anything!" I lifted my leg up over my head.

His blue eyes darted over toward me. "Now you're

just being a tease."

∞

The pool hall wasn't much more than a smoky bar that looked like an oversized green trailer.

"You promise we can go somewhere to be alone after this?" I pouted out my bottom lip as Blaine closed the door to his truck behind me.

He leaned both his hands against the truck, on either side of me, and pressed his forehead to mine. "I promise tonight won't be a waste of your heels." He looked down at my chest. "Or your push-up bra."

"Hey, I am not wearing a push-up bra!"

He grinned at me, we were eye level, and I was almost even taller.

"Libby, I've known you a month now, and after staring at your chest just about every day that I've known you, I think I know when you have a push-up bra on." He nuzzled my cheek in an attempt to muffle his laugh.

"Damn boy, finally you make it!" A short stocky guy in a backwards red hat smacked the back of Blaine's head, causing Blaine to knock forward. He caught himself with his hands before our heads butted.

"Well damn, I think if I had a girl like that I would probably have taken even longer," a really tall black guy in a Tulane shirt chimed in.

"Come on guys." A guy that looked about five years older than the rest of them with a full red beard put his arm around the other two boys. "Give Blaine a break. We've already cock blocked him enough."

Blaine turned toward the three guys, sliding an arm around my waist. "Alright now that you've embarrassed the hell out of me, meet my girlfriend, Libby."

He pointed to the short stocky guy. "Libby, that's Ryan, we played baseball together in high school." He then pointed toward the tall black guy. "That's Don, he thinks he's too good for us now that he goes to Tulane, but we can still kick his ass."

"Hey!" Don chimed. For a black guy he had a really high sing-songy voice. I didn't think he was at Tulane on any sort of a sports scholarship with a voice like that.

"Really Don, you can't deny it." The third guy looked at Don, and then extended his hand toward me, trying to grab my attention with his eyes. "And I'm Jackson. I've worked with Blaine on the road crew for forever."

"Yeah that's why he's good at the wise cracks, he's had centuries to practice them," Don quipped.

"Hey!" He turned back to Don. "I'm not too old to still kick your ass."

"Bring it on old balls!" Don made a motion with his hands like, come and get me.

"You got it choir boy!" Jackson went straight for Don's knees. Before I knew it the two were wrestling in the parking lot.

That only lasted about 30 seconds though, before Blaine broke it up.

"Come on guys, let's play some pool."

∞

Now being in college, and having an older sister that I could pass off as, of course I had a fake ID. But in a small town bar, I don't think I was carded even once. The boys ordered rounds of beers at the pool table, and I don't think the waitress even batted an eye.

It could take a bit to get me drunk, especially with beer, but after about four beers I was feeling pretty tipsy. I was trying to point the stick straight, Blaine was behind me trying to show me how to aim the cue.

"I bet you Blaine is used to seeing her from this position." Ryan cackled and the rest of the boys joined in. I think they had a few even before they came.

Blaine whispered in my ear. "Shh don't listen to them, we're losing pretty bad, I'll help you make this shot."

I whispered back, slurring a bit. "Then will you make a shot on me?"

I guess it wasn't that much of a whisper because Jackson yelled, "I HEARD SHOTS."

I totally fumbled with the cue stick and cracked the cue into the ball, making it ricochet off of the side of the table. I just laughed like a drunken school girl falling onto the table along with my cue stick.

"Oh shit," Don muttered.

"What?" Blaine took his hands off of me and looked to the side. Then I could feel his steel grip on my back. Something he saw made him very angry.

"What is she doing here?" He spat between clenched teeth.

I slowly got up from the table to look and see what all the boys were staring at.

Two girls sat at a small table across from the bar.

One of them was really pretty and petite, something I would never be. She had almost all small features, except for a ginormous rack, which she made sure to show off with a very low cut shirt. Her hair was very straight and brown, I envied that with humidity. She took tiny sips out of her drink in a rocks glass and laughed with the girl next to her.

"Five Tequila shots." The little mousy waitress squealed holding a tray in the middle of us. The boys were snapped out of their stare fest to turn their attention to the waitress.

Jackson plopped a fifty on the tray. "Keep em' coming."

I got out the salt shaker and began to pour it on the back of my hand, but before I could even finish Blaine had taken his shot, not waiting for the salt or to take the lime afterwards.

"I'm going to step outside for a minute." He patted my back, and just continued out to the door without even looking at me.

I whirled around and turned toward the guys, who were huddled together talking. "Um, did I miss something?"

"Uh..." Ryan just froze.

"Well?" Don broke away from the group and came closer toward me. "See the little brunette over at the table with the big red head." I glanced over my shoulder, pretending to pick something off of my shoulder and saw that the brunette was doing the same thing. She quickly turned back toward her friend in order to not make eye contact with me.

"Yeah." I turned back toward Don. "What about her?"

"Well." He rubbed the back of his clean shaven head. "That would be Julie, Blaine's ex."

Oh, wow.

Ryan scooted in between us with Jackson close on his heels. "Yeah I thought that bitch said she'd never come around here again."

"Well I guess we'll just have to make sure she knows what she's been missing." I didn't bother licking the salt off of my hand and downed the shot, motioning to the waitress for another.

Blaine finally came back in after about my fourth or fifth shot. I had kind of lost count. I really wasn't expecting Julie to be that pretty, and I was hoping Blaine wasn't having second thoughts about me after seeing her again.

"Hey Blainey!" I slurred, jumping into Blaine's arms when he came back to the table. "I was afraid you would never come back!" I swayed back in forth in his arms, holding him tight.

"Um, Libby are you okay?" Blaine pulled me away and held my eyes with his. I noticed his eyes were blood shot. I didn't know what he had been doing outside, but whatever it was, I figured this Julie bitch had to pay.

"Honey, can you go get me a drink?" I drew a circle on his chest with my finger.

"Are you sure you need another drink?" He kept trying to lock eye contact with me, but I wouldn't let him.

"Please, honey. No more beer though, rum and Coke?" I gave him the puppy dog eyes, batting my eyelashes in the process, a double whammy.

He groaned. "Fine, I'll be right back." He let go of

me and headed toward the bar.

That was my chance, if I ever had one; I probably had enough liquid courage in me to really do something stupid.

"I'll be back boys." I called without even looking back at Marcus, Ryan, and Don.

Slowly I slunk my way over to the table where Julie and her friend were sitting. For a moment I just stood there in front of him. The girls stopped their conversation. Julie just looked at me with her top lip curled up in a look of disgust.

"Um, can I help you?" Ugh, even her voice was cute, like something a teenage country singer would have.

I smirked. I hadn't gotten as far as to thinking what I was going to say.

"Um, hello?" The girl sitting next to her questioned, trying not to laugh. I probably looked like an idiot, a giant blonde idiot.

"Hi." I squeaked and thrusted my hand out to the two girls. "I don't think we've met, I'm Libby Gentry, Dee Badeaux's niece. I just moved here about a month ago and well." I shrugged with that shit eating grin still plastered on my face. "I thought with it being a pretty small town I'd met everyone here, but I guess I haven't."

"Oh, well I'm Dani and this is my friend Julie, but she doesn't live around here anymore. She just came to visit for the night from New Orleans." The chubby redhead said in the friendliest voice she could utter. She was definitely Julie's wingman, or wing woman, if there is such a thing.

"Oh, Julie." I turned my body completely toward

her. "Yeah I think you know my boyfriend, Blaine Crabtree."

"Uh, yeah." Julie took a drink of her drink and rolled her eyes. "Come on Dani, I think it's getting a bit crowded in here." Julie grabbed her purse and began to stand.

Here was my turn to make an even bigger ass of myself. I slammed my hand down on their table and that startled both of them to sit back down. "I'm sorry? Did I just crowd your space or was that some sort of a tall joke?"

"Um excuse me?" Julie put her tongue in her cheek and crossed her arms, shooting lasers at me with her dark green eyes.

The room was spinning. I leaned in, and I thought I could almost see Julie cringe at the smell of Tequila on my breath.

"Listen bitch, you may be prettier than me and have better hair."

Julie smirked at that.

"But I know I am a hell of a lot better dresser than you and make Blaine a hell of a lot happier than you ever could." I leaned in even closer, a definite invasion of personal space. "And if I ever see you or your fake ass Chanel earrings around here again, I will shove my very real, very pointy Jimmy Choos up your prissy little ass. Do I make myself clear?"

Julie opened her mouth to say something, but the quickly closed it. I think she knew in my state I would probably do something stupid. I got up from the table and turned toward the guys. Jackson, Don, and Marcus were all staring at me in amazement, but Blaine was just shaking his head. I tried to walk back over to them with some swagger. Then the worst thing that could happen, happened. I felt my heel get caught in the wooden planks of the floor, and then it all went dark.

∞

I woke up with my head pressed against the glass of Blaine's truck. My head was throbbing. I opened one eye and could see Blaine just staring out the window, a clove in his hand. He knew I didn't like him smoking, so he tried not to do it around me. But just from his body language, blank stare, and hand gripped on the wheel, I knew he was pretty upset.

I slowly sat up in the seat, still holding my head and groaning loudly. I opened both eyes slowly and looked out the front window. I didn't recognize where we were at all. I just knew it wasn't the bar or either of our houses.

"Mmmm...Where are we?" I rubbed the back of my head. I could feel a big knot where my hand was.

"Real nice, Libby. You see my ex in a bar and decide to cause a scene. I mean, that's class right there." Blaine didn't even look at me, just took that long slow last drag of his clove and then tossed the butt out the window.

I rubbed my head and shifted my body completely toward Blaine, very slowly, but eventually my whole body was facing him, with my hand still on the back of my head.

"You make a scene in a bar." Blaine finally turned his attention toward me, his eyes were that same angry steel blue. "Not only do you go and talk to my ex-girlfriend, but then you threaten her. It wouldn't have been so bad, that is, if your drunk ass didn't fall on the floor and pass out."

My memory was starting to come back. I remember falling and Blaine's friends cheering me on. Then I remember a man coming over and telling Blaine to get his drunk-ass girlfriend out of the bar and not to bring her back. From there I didn't remember anything else.

"I had to carry you out of the bar, with everyone staring." He practically spat. "Do you know how embarrassing that was for me? What if your Aunt Dee finds out, or even worse, my parents?"

"Blaine, I was just..." I stammered.

"You were just what?" He clenched his teeth. "Trying to embarrass me in front of my ex? Make it even worse for me?" His knuckles were almost white since his hands were gripped so hard onto the steering wheel. "I'm sure she really thinks highly of you, slobbering all over her. That really makes her think I'm moving up in the world."

I didn't know what else to do or to say and I was still pretty drunk, so I did the only thing I could do. I cried. Oh, and not a pretty cry, It was an all-out sob. My tears were black from my makeup and snot dripped out of my nose.

Blaine took his hands off the wheel and pulled my toward him, burying my face in his chest. "Baby, don't cry." He ran his fingers through my hair, which was a big fluffy mess from the humidity and falling down in the bar.

"I'm...I'm...SORRY," I blurted between sniffles.

"Shhh. Libby, it's okay." He kissed the top of my

head. "It was kind of funny, you should have seen the look on her face."

I looked up at Blaine, my face completely tear streaked. I wiped my nose with the back of my hand. "Are you still mad at me?" I blabbered.

Blaine groaned. "I don't know if I can stay mad at you when you pull the crying card."

"Hmmm." I traced my fingers down his shirt to the top of his pants. "Maybe I should do that more often then."

He stroked my cheek. "Well I hope I'm not making you cry all the time."

"Hey, I did get my alone time though." I slowly undid his belt buckle.

"Libby. Do you really think this is the time or the place?"

I reached my head closer to his. "I think you need to stop thinking." Then I closed his mouth with my own and enveloped him into a kiss.

∞

Well we both didn't think our first time together should be in the front seat of his car, but I really thought that I should make up my stupidness of the night to him.

"Libby, I don't think we should be doing this out here." Blaine stammered, trying his best to keep his attention away from me.

"Come on Blaine. We are out in the middle of nowhere and no one will have to find out." I looked up at him, batting my eyelashes and pursing my lips.

"Well...if you insist..." He grinned.

I tried to lean back, but realized that I was caught. Okay I was actually, really caught and something was pulling on my hair.

"OW." I screeched as I furiously started yanking my head back and forth.

"What the hell, Libby?" Blaine's eyes widened as he lifted his arms in the air.

"I'm caught on something." I stammered, finally stopping to inspect what I was caught on.

Blaine looked down and covered his mouth, trying to stifle his laughter. "Honey, your hair is caught on my belt buckle."

I looked down to see a big chunk of my hair wrapped around his bright green John Deere belt buckle.

"Ack!" I waved my arms in the air, like I was scratching at nothing. "Get it out, get it out!"

He laughed again, but this time he stifled it quicker. "Alright baby, calm down." He put his hand on the top of my head. "Now you are going to have to lean back down, so I'm not ripping your hair out."

I leaned my head back down on his lap as Blaine finagled with the belt buckle, trying to pull out the blonde strands without hurting me.

"Oh shit." he mumbled.

"What?" I looked up, hoping not to see a huge clump of my hair in his hands.

"COP. COP. COP." Blaine screamed as he stared into his rearview mirror.

I tried to lift my head up, but then he pushed it back down, hitting the exact spot I had hit on the floor at the bar on the steering wheel. "OW!" I screeched, ripping that last piece of my hair out of Blaine's belt buckle.

"Aw baby I'm sorry." He kissed the top of my head quickly and tried to straighten out his belt.

I slinked over to my side of the seat. "I thought you said we were pretty far off the beaten path and that no one would find us."

"Well I thought we were!" He was shaking as he fiddled with his belt buckle.

"What are we going to do?" I was still drunk and was crouched up on the seat on all fours like a cat. My face was still completely black and tear streaked. I could only imagine what my hair looked like.

Blaine shook his head and was actually laughing. The cop was still sitting in the car behind us with his lights on and Blaine was laughing his ass off.

"Blaine, what's so damn funny?" I spat between gritted teeth.

"You know in the time we've been together, we've been stopped by the cops twice. I think that's a first." He nodded his head like he was proud of himself.

"Well I'm sorry, but I don't think it's funny that there is a cop behind us and we may have just got caught for public indecency."

"Baby." He reached for my hand and gave me an encouraging smile. "Relax, it'll be fine."

He didn't smile for too long as the cop tapped on the window.

Blaine held never let go of my hand as he turned toward the window and rolled it down.

"Hello officer, is everything alright?" The sexy boyfriend hat was immediately off and on came that southern charm.

The police officer looked like a typical small town

police officer: a little overweight, a little gray, but a perfect handlebar mustache.

"Evening Blaine, out a little late isn't you two?" The cop leaned in against the window, and then nodded in my direction. "Miss Gentry, good to see you again, maybe I'll get to see you someday not pulled over."

Great, it was the same cop that we saw with my high and drunk little cousin. I had to be making the best impression on the Elsbury police department.

"Now I heard," The cop turned his attention back toward to Blaine, leaning his body against the car door and smacking his lips as he talked. "That there was some sort of a scene at Reesey's that involved the Doddery girl." The officer raised his eyebrows at the mention of Julie's name.

Blaine squeezed my hand lightly. "Well, you know them city girls, Officer Campbell." Blaine threw a smile my way and then looked back at the officer. "Well especially this one in particular." He threw his head back in my direction. "They've got a bit of a temper."

I wanted to pipe up and say something, but I just bit down on my lip, not even moving from my crouching tiger position.

The officer laughed at that and Blaine joined in. "Well, the Doddery girl was none too happy. She wanted to press charges, but everyone there agreed that Julie had started it all and Libby there never raised a hand to her."

The cop leaned his head in closer. "Julie didn't like that too much. I don't think we'll see her around these parts again."

"Good to hear Officer Campbell. Good to hear."

Blaine squeezed my hand again.

"But," Officer Campbell continued. "I can't just turn a blind eye to you getting a little...you know..." He put a fist to his mouth and stuck his tongue into his cheek, moving his fist back and forth. "From your girlfriend out here in the swamp."

I was still drunk and tried not to laugh at the hand gesture the cop made. I tightly covered my mouth with one hand and leaned my shoulder against the seat, so I wouldn't fall over.

I didn't hear much more of what they said after that. I don't think they wanted me to know either. They lowered their voices and Officer Campbell did a lot of nodding and glancing over at me. And within about twenty minutes the two men were laughing and the cop was letting us go.

"Now you behave yourself Miss Gentry, next time I see you I don't want it to be because I'm in the cop car, ya hear?"

My eyes were so droopy that I could barely keep them open as I nodded to Officer Campbell.

"Alright now." Office Campbell nodded profusely. "Mr. Crabtree, get this young lady home, we don't want Aunt Dee up all night waiting for her." He patted Blaine on the shoulder and then got in his car and left.

Blaine leaned in and kissed my half open eyes. "We really need to stop seeing Officer Campbell like this."

"And you really need to not let me wear stilettos."

CHAPTER 15

Fourth of July in a small town is kind of a big deal. Aunt Dee closed the shop down for the day as people lined the streets for the annual parade and fair. Fourth of July had to be kind of a bittersweet day for Aunt Dee. I knew it was the day that everything changed for her daughter. But if she was upset she didn't let anyone see it. She was busy baking pies for the fair and handing out flags for everyone in town.

"What are you and Blaine doing today?" Aunt Dee questioned when I strolled out of the bedroom. She had already been up since the break of dawn baking.

"I think we are going to his friend Jackson's or something." I yawned, shrugging at the end of a big stretch. The truth of the matter was absolutely nothing had still happened with Blaine and I, and I think things had gotten worse since the night at the bar.

Every time I had even tried anything more than making out, Blaine would immediately stop everything all together. Today was the day I was hoping to change all of that. I spent almost an entire paycheck ordering new lingerie from Agent Provocateur, a website that Kristi introduced me for when she was looking for her wedding night outfit. I practically had to tackle the mail man to get to it before Aunt Dee saw it.

"Oh, is Brittany going with you?" Aunt Dee looked up at me from behind those Coke bottle glasses.

Oh Brittany. Blaine insisted that she hang out with us even more. If there was a female word for cock block, Britt would be it. Between her sitting in the living room with us every time we'd watch TV, to Aunt Dee sitting at the table scrapbooking if Britt was gone for the night.

I shrugged again. "I don't know. I guess if she wants to."

"Brittany go where?" Britt shuffled out of her bedroom, rubbing her eyes. My mission to turn her into more of a girl was failing miserably. She was clad in an oversized t-shirt and some basketball shorts. I bought her some pink pajamas at one point, but I think she just threw them in the back of her closet.

"Oh, Brittany, you're awake." Aunt Dee glanced quickly at Britt, but then went back to mixing something in a large blue bowl. "Libby was just telling me that she and Blaine were going over to that Cleary boy's house for the Fourth of July. Were you planning on going too?"

"Jackson's having a party?" Britt's eyes perked up as she leaped into the kitchen.

"Uh, yeah. I guess he is." Shit just what I needed, Britt tagging along.

"I've got the softball game this afternoon" Britt reached a chubby finger into one of Aunt Dee's mixing bowls, coming up with a big dollop of dough and scooping it into her mouth. "I think Sarah may be having a party too. Her dad got a bunch of fireworks this year and last year her brother blew up a toad with a bottle rocket."

"Ew, I think that was probably unnecessary." I wrinkled my nose, but secretly smiled. Maybe I would be able to get Blaine away from Jackson's too. I knew Aunt Dee's house would be empty since she would be so busy with the fair and parade, and Blaine's house would definitely be empty.

Thank God. For a minute there I thought it might be a perfectly good waste of new panties.

∞

Aunt Dee spent the rest of the early morning baking, and then quickly packed up her car to make it to the antique shop in time for the parade. The parade didn't officially start till ten, so Britt and I had some time to lie around the house.

"So what did you get from that Agent place?" Britt peered over at me from behind the couch.

I stopped scrubbing the dish I had in the sink. "Uh, you know just the essentials, panties and the like." I nodded to myself thinking that answer was sufficient, and finished scrubbing the last of the dozens of dishes Aunt Dee left behind. I didn't know if I could ever do the baking thing if it took that many dishes.

"So nothing kinky like edible underwear or nipple guards or something?" Britt got up on her knees and leaned in with her elbows propped up on the edge of the couch.

I wiped my hands with a spare dish towel and walked into the living room. "I don't think Agent Provocateur even sells those kinds of things, perv." I threw the dish towel at her face.

"Hey." She took the dish towel off her face throwing it to the side. "Well, I heard." She scooted down so that she was sitting on the couch next to me, just as I sat down. "That you got caught giving Blaine a blow job off of Parrish road last week."

My jaw dropped. How the hell did she know that? Even more so it wasn't even a blow job, but more of a me-looking-stupid-job.

"Where did you hear that from?" I tried to remain calm, but my hands were balling up into fists.

Britt rolled her eyes. "Come on Libby, don't tell me you haven't learned anything while you've been living here. It's a small town. We hear it all."

I guess that would explain why Dina and Marion were giving me such weird looks and would giggle every time I would tell Blaine that I was hungry.

"Okay, now I'm sufficiently embarrassed. I mean we didn't even do anything, but does everyone think that we did?" I tussled my hair with a free hand and curled my feet under my knees.

"Probably." Britt bobbed her head up and down repeatedly. "The other night at Sarah's one of the guys had referred to you as Libby Lips."

"GROSS!" I shrieked. "I think that's even worse than Big Bird!" I shook my hair about like I was trying to get a bug out of it. "I wonder if Blaine knows what people are saying."

Britt shrugged. "I don't know, but I'll let you deal with that one." She patted my knee and then got up from the couch. "I'm going to go take a shower before you hog it for the rest of the morning."

"Hey use my new shampoo; it will make your hair

grow faster. I promise!" I yelled as Britt walked out of the room.

"Yeah. Yeah." She yelled back from behind the closed bathroom door.

I grabbed my phone and quickly dialed Blaine's number. It rang, and rang, I thought he was never going to pick up.

"Hullo?" He sounded like he had just woken up, his voice was groggy like it was killing him just to answer.

"Blaine do you know what people are saying about us?" I shrieked into the phone like a nervous school girl.

"Baby," he groaned. I could hear his muscles stretch and pop in the background. "Did you know its seven a.m. and not a work day?"

"I'm serious!" I sat straight up, thinking maybe somehow my posture would emphasize my words better. "Britt said that everyone knows about you and me and the truck the other night."

"So?" He yawned.

"So? SO? Is that all you have to say? We get caught by the police with my head stuck in your crotch and all you have to say is so?" I got up and paced back and forth in the living room.

I heard him groan again and his bed creak. I could tell he was slowly getting up. "It's not like we got arrested for it. Besides, technically, we weren't doing anything wrong. Like you said, you just got stuck."

The shower turned on in the bathroom, water started slowly spraying a steady stream. Good, Britt wouldn't be able to hear our conversation.

"Blaine, Britt said some guy at Sarah's called me

Libby Lips!"

Blaine actually laughed. "Are you serious?"

"It's not funny." I pouted, putting my free hand on my hip.

"I'm sorry Libby. I know it's not."

"Then why did you laugh?"

He groaned again. "Well what do you want me to do?"

"I think you should get caught going down on me in the swamp and get a nickname like Blowy Blaine, or something."

I heard the air blow through his nose as he smiled. "Do you want me to come over there and go down on you in the swamp?"

"Yes. Yes I do."

"Alright." He cracked his back. "I'll be over in about an hour to take you to the parade. I'll even wear the John Deere belt buckle just for you." I heard him smile again.

"That's not funny."

He groaned, "Baby..."

"Okay, fine. See you soon." I muttered.

"Bye babe."

I hung up the phone and sprawled back on the couch. Brittany would only take about ten minutes in the shower, and I figured I would probably need as much time as I could in there when she was done.

∞

Blaine was, of course, early as usual. I had barely finished doing my hair and was just standing in the bathroom in a tank top and shorts when he walked in.

He waltzed in the house without even knocking and just stood in the doorway of the bathroom.

"Is that what you are wearing today?" He leaned in on the door frame.

"Actually I planned on just being naked, and then you could have better access to my goodies. I thought maybe we could do this during the parade." I turned away from the mirror and smirked at him, shaking what little of a chest I had.

"Ew, please don't go naked." Brittany piped in, squeezing between Blaine and the doorframe. "I've already got the cousin with the loose lips, I don't want to have the cousin with the loose everything."

Blaine laughed and I shot him an evil glare.

"Fine." I locked in on Brittany's' eyes. "I'll wear clothes only if you change yours."

"What's wrong with what I'm wearing?" She quipped holding out the bottom of her sleeveless red shirt, her freckles arms were almost the same color as the shirt.

"Too many things to name."

"Fine!" She stomped into her room.

"Did you make me breakfast?" Blaine leaned in and kissed me hard on the lips.

"No. Do I look like I've been cooking?"

Blaine put his arms around my waist and lifted me up off the ground, twirling me around until we were in the hallway. "How do you expect to become a true southern belle if you can't cook?" He kissed me again and then put me down.

"By marrying a rich southern man of course!" I stuck my tongue out at him.

"Don't tease Libby Lips!" He tickled my sides while

I squirmed and giggled against his hands.

"You two are disgusting!" Britt wrinkled her nose as she walked back into the living room. She was dressed much better this time. She was actually wearing the jean capris and paired it with a tiered blue tank top that I just happened to find on clearance one day.

I pulled away from Blaine's grip and stood in front of him, patrolling my eyes up and down Britt's outfit. "Much better!" I clapped.

"Now will you put on clothes?" She rolled her eyes.

"Will you put on a headband to match your outfit?" I leaned my head in hoping it would be a yes.

"Um, no. I got this far, and I think that's far enough for today."

"Makeup?" I steepled my fingers together in front of my face.

"No. Now get dressed." She pointed toward my bedroom.

"And Blaine." She turned to him as I started toward the bedroom. "You stay here. I don't want to hear anything I don't need to from the bedroom."

"I can try and be quiet!" I yelled, poking my head out the door.

"Yeah, but I can't be." Blaine yelled back.

"EW." Brittany screeched.

Some days, actually most days, I wished Blaine would actually do what he says, instead of just joke about it.

Since Britt and I's only ride to the parade was in Blaine's truck, we were pretty much packed in like sardines. At least Britt was since I made her sit in the back.

"Why do I have to sit in the back?" She protested, crossing her arms over her chest.

"Because I have long legs and they are hard to get in the back of the truck." I traced a finger down my long legs. Thank God they were at least tanning nicely in the Louisiana sun or I would look like a giant thing of string cheese.

"I bet you Blaine could get you in the back of the truck." She rolled her head from side to side.

Blaine swooped an arm around me. "I probably could, but this isn't the time or the place." He shot a quick smile at me then looked back at Britt. "Now can you just please get in the back of the truck so we can get going?"

"Fine!" Britt threw her hands up in the air and then reluctantly climbed into the backseat of the truck.

I grabbed Blaine's wrist and pulled him back toward me before he could walk around to the driver's side. My lips traced along his earlobe as I whispered. "Just because I'm in a dress today doesn't mean I'll be getting in the back of the truck."

He turned and kissed the bottom of my jaw line then whispered in my ear. "We'll see about that one."

I didn't return the smile and sighed. "Sometimes I wish you would just stop joking and actually just do it."

"Patience, baby." He yelled and got into his side of the truck. "Patience."

We rode pretty much in silence except for the extremely terrible music that Blaine listened to. Britt seemed to enjoy it, but I constantly tried to change his

CD or even put on the radio. Not to mention, I was even more uncomfortable with what I was wearing underneath my dress. I had on nothing more than just a strapless red dress, which was made of a cotton material, with a bubble hem. It was still more uncomfortable than anything when you are wearing lace underneath cotton. All I wanted to do was scratch my nether regions, but I thought people might think something was wrong with me.

The downtown area was packed. I think the entire Parrish decided to come to the parade. All three blocks of downtown were lined with people in folded chairs, kids screaming from on top of their father's shoulders, and lots of American flags in every shop window, and every person's hand or wagon. Aunt Dee said we could park in the back of the shop, so at least that helped us for a parking spot. Britt tumbled out of the car as soon as we go to the office.

"FREEDOM!" She almost screamed and ran out of the truck to go find her friends.

Blaine came around to the other side of the car and reached for my hand. I took it and pulled him back so he was facing me while I leaned against the passenger side door. "Are we going to get some alone time that's not just in your truck today?"

"Well I can't promise anything Libby, but we can sure try." His southern accent just poured out like syrup, it was so sugary sweet.

"I feel like you've been avoiding it for some time now, and I just thought, I mean nobody is at my Aunt Dee's almost all day today." I traced my finger in circles on his chest. How I wished I could just see him minus the shirt. "We can even ditch the parade now and go over there."

He pushed my hand down off of his chest. He was so close I could feel some movement in his pants. "Not here babe." He kissed my forehead. "Come on, it's your first Elsbury Fourth of July parade. It'll be fun."

Fun was not the word I was thinking. He took my hand again and we headed toward the front of the office hand in hand.

"Oh, y'all finally made it!" Aunt Dee grabbed Blaine and me, embracing us into a hug.

"Not everyone can be up at the crack of dawn like your family, but Libby's trying to get me to be." Blaine beamed at Aunt Dee when she let us go.

"Well Dee, I think you may have another southern belle after all." One of Aunt Dee's friends piped in. I recognized her as Maize Thibodaux, one of Aunt Dee's friends from bridge club, whose husband owned one of the grocery stores in town.

"Libby?" Blaine almost couldn't contain his laughter, which I didn't understand because he was always joking about me being a southern belle.

"Why yes, Mr. Crabtree." Maize put her hand out like she was swatting a fly. "I mean just look at her."

I twirled a piece of my hair. The only thing that came to my mind when I thought of a southern belle was Scarlett O'Hara.

"Nails polished, her hair done, and even with a headband to match her shoes! She looks like she could just go right out now and make her Debut!" Maize clasped her hands together.

"Oh, well I think Libby's a bit old for that." Aunt Dee looked down. "But Brittany does turn sixteen next year." She grimaced.

Maize patted Aunt Dee's shoulder and smirked before they went back to their bright green lawn chairs near the edge of the street.

Thank God I watched a lot of television, or I'd have no idea what they were talking about. A Debut was a big ordeal I guess in some parts of the south, though I did not think in small town Louisiana it was a big deal. It was kind of like a coming of age for girls just to say 'I'm here and I'm pretty and I'm a southern lady!' I kind of had the feeling that Blaine's ex was probably one of these girls that made her debut, and I also thought that Britt was probably one of those girls who never would.

"I told you that you were her hope for a southern belle." Blaine whispered as he stood behind me.

I turned my head back toward him and looked up. "You know you're lucky I'm wearing flat sandals today, or you wouldn't be able to see the parade over my hair."

"Maybe you should work on taming the blonde beast."

"At least it's natural. Well mostly anyways."

"Touché." He kissed the top of my head.

The parade went on just as I thought every small town parade would. Complete with floats from the local high school, fire engines, and ending with a convertible carrying the mayor and the local fair queen. They all traveled down that little narrow strip of downtown, some floats even getting caught on the pot holes that I'm sure Blaine was thinking needed to be filled. Nothing too exciting, but I think Aunt Dee was happy to have me there. It was truly her last happy memory of Joni, having her as the fair queen.

I couldn't even imagine what was going through her mind. Was she happy to be at the fair, or did she want to cry seeing the fair queen so happy and waving at the crowd? I knew she loved Britt, but I also wonder if she ever imagined what it would have been like if Joni would have never had Britt, and that night would have never happened.

Britt was nowhere to be found as Blaine and I walked down to the high school, which was literally about one hundred yards from the downtown, where they had the fair set out on the grounds. There were a few rides, a bunch of craft and bake sale booths, and complete with a big stage where a lot of amateur talent played.

"Blaine, why don't you get up there and play something?" I asked between slurps of a lemon shake up.

"Naw, that's not really my thing." He squinted while we walked around the perimeter of the fair.

"Why not? I think you're pretty good."

"Yeah, but you're my girlfriend, you're supposed to say that." He gently squeezed my hand.

I wanted to say, and you're my boyfriend you're supposed to want to screw me. But I didn't, I just kept walking.

"Well, Britt's softball game has probably started, did you want to go watch?" He asked

I didn't want to. I really just wanted to get my dress off and roll around in the sheets with Blaine, but the Fourth of July festival was definitely not the place to be doing that.

"Yeah." I forced a weak smile.

"C'mon I'll show you to the fields. You know I used to play in high school right?" He swung our interlocked hands back and forth while we walked.

I shook my head. "No, you actually never told me that." But by his biceps I could tell he had to do something.

"Yup, All-Parrish pitcher my senior year." He said proudly.

"Do you still play?"

"Well..." He ran a free hand through his hair. "There is a summer league that some of the guys threw together, but I haven't really had time."

I knew that meant between work and spending most nights with me, it wouldn't fit in. I didn't know if I should feel bad about him not playing, but he answered that for me.

"Besides, if I were playing ball when would I get to spend time with you?" He grinned, letting go of my hand and putting his arm around my shoulders.

"You shouldn't really stop doing something you like just because of someone else," I muttered under my breath.

I never realized how many things I stopped doing just because I'd wanted to spend more time with Beau or with my Kappa sisters. Things that I used to love were suddenly too uncool, and I stopped caring about them. Like the saxophone, I used to love to be in jazz band in school. I played the saxophone so much that my dad built me my own little studio in the basement, so that he wouldn't have to hear me playing all the time.

But when you are in a sorority it isn't cool to be a band nerd, and when your mom asks why you don't play for her anymore, you have to lie. Or when you have to lie that you love your classes, when really you never show up for them. I didn't know who I became over the school year, but I definitely did not like who that girl was anymore, and was hoping Blaine wouldn't become someone he hated for me.

"Hey, there's Britt," he called, pointing toward the softball diamond.

It was not even a block from the school and hordes of girls were running around, throwing balls back and forth. Britt, of course, was squatting down with all her catcher's gear in place. Who would have guessed she would be the catcher? I was starting to feel like a big hypocrite now, insisting that she wear what I wanted her to, but somehow it was okay for Blaine not to play baseball because of me. That just wasn't fair of me to think that way, and I felt terrible.

"Hey Blaine!" A petite little redhead came running over to the fence.

Immediately I tensed up and put my arm tighter around Blaine's waist. It wasn't enough that I was always worried about other girls. Now I was just paranoid.

"Hey Sadie." He beamed walking toward the fence.

"Hey, our umpire got some kind of stomach flu, would you mind stepping in?" She pointed a thumb toward home plate.

No, please say no, please say no.

"Sure." He cracked a huge smile. "You don't mind, do you baby?" He looked down at me. I could see the pleading in those baby blues. How could I say no?

"Yeah, go ahead." He beamed letting go of me. "Have fun!" I yelled as he jogged to the other side of the fence.

I found a seat on the bleachers in-between the crazy softball moms that had gathered and dads with their video cameras.

"Libby, is that you?"

Great, I'd been spotted. Maize Thibodaux came scooting down next to me at the end of the bleachers.

"Hi Mrs. Thibodaux." I grimaced.

"Why, where is Blaine?" She fanned herself with a free hand, her dark gray eyes peering around the park.

Maize Thibodaux was not an attractive woman by any means. It was like a bunch of cow licks got together and decided to have a big party in her curly gray hair. And if her hair wasn't bad enough, that bad hair framed her chubby face, complete with beady little gray eyes, and enough moles and freckles to start an army. But she prided herself on being a southern debutante, from what I later learned, she ran the yearly Cotillion at the country club a few towns over. Even though she was about 100 pounds overweight she still carried herself like she was a debutante herself.

"Oh, they needed an umpire, so he's helping out." I leaned back onto the seats behind me, thinking I'd at least be able to get somewhat of a tan today.

"Oh, why look at that." She squinted toward home plate. "You know I haven't seen him on a field since high school! Did he tell you that he was All-Parrish? And even pitched for the state team."

I nodded. If I didn't know something in this town, leave it to little gossiping old ladies to let me know.

"I honestly think that's the only reason that

Doddery girl stayed with him so long." She wiped a big glob of sweat off of her brow.

"Now I don't like to speak ill of people usually, but for being a debutante, that girl was the most stuck-up little thing I had ever met."

"Really now?" I leaned in a bit more. I couldn't help it if it was good gossip, and it was about Blaine's ex, I had to hear it.

"Oh yes. Always walking around like she was better than anyone else just because her daddy was a lawyer. Well you don't see him practicing law in this town anymore do you?"

She nodded with satisfaction.

"Anyways, when a girl makes her debut, one of the most important things is her escort. The man who introduces you, shows your place in society, and I remember Julie had said she didn't want just any good ol' boy to escort her. If it wasn't for Blaine being the star pitcher, I don't think she would have even stayed with him. It was all about wearing his letterman jacket for her and the prize that came along with that."

I knew girls like that in high school, dating the star football player and suddenly their shit didn't stink. I wondered if Blaine ever realized that's why Julie was with him, it wasn't like I was going to say anything to him though. I'm sure in high school he wouldn't have even looked at me. I'm sure if the kids in my high school looked at me now they wouldn't believe it. The band nerd and a baseball player became the sorority girl and the road crew grunt, and now they're dating. Who would have thought?

It seemed like we were there for HOURS. Even

though the games were only seven innings long, Blaine decided to umpire for all three games. I sat there trying to smile. If this was what made him happy, then maybe he wouldn't mind making me happy later.

Finally he shook hands with all the girls on both teams, and was thanked profusely with a little too many hugs by the redhead, before he came back running over toward me.

"So you ready to go over to Jackson's place?" Blaine asked placing a big sweaty kiss on my forehead, that I quickly wiped away.

I couldn't find Britt anywhere, and figured maybe this would actually give us some alone time if she didn't tag along. I turned to look for Mrs. Thibodaux, but it looked like she had already left too, it was just as well.

"Sure." I shrugged. "I think I've had my fill of this thing for now".

∞

Jackson lived more out in the boondocks than Aunt Dee's or Blaine's place. It was a small blue house, I guess you could almost call it a shack. But the land it was on was beautiful. It was a large plot of land with a lake in the back, or maybe it was a creek, I failed geography in college too.

When we pulled out to the gravel path, there were already a bunch of guys out on the front lawn, most of them in their swim trunks and probably all of them were at least halfway to being plastered.

"HEY BLAINE'S HERE!" Ryan ran over to the truck

as Blaine closed the door behind me.

"Oh Libby, thank God you aren't wearing heels! I don't want you to attack me on my fashion!" He grinned putting an arm around me. "I'm just kidding with you."

He burped, it smelled like cheap beer and crawfish, I had to turn away. "Now come on you two, go get into your suits and grab a beer!" Ryan let go of me and then headed back over to a couple of guys that were playing bags over to the side of the house.

"It may not exactly be one of your sorority parties." Blaine started, but I turned and put a finger on his lips.

"Its fine baby, come with me to go change." I took my finger off of his lips and grabbed his hand.

"You brought a swimsuit?" He cocked an eyebrow trailing behind me.

"No, um." I tried to speed up as he was slacking behind. "But I don't want to just strip off my dress in front of everyone." At least that got him to shut up for a while.

We had to stop another ten times it felt like, for people to stop and drunkenly say hi to Blaine or to high five him, or for me to be introduced to another person I had probably already met twenty times before. I just really wanted to get Blaine alone. Finally, after what seemed like forever, I got him back in what must have been Jackson's bedroom.

It was near the back end of the house, so it was kind of dark. The walls were painted gray and the room wasn't furnished with much more than a huge waterbed covered with a dark blue bedspread.

"So...where is..." Blaine walked toward the edge of

the room as I shut the door behind us.

While his back was turned to me, I slowly slipped off my dress. He turned just as I slid the top down to show my chest popping out of the black lace merry widow.

"Um." Blaine's eyes widened as he couldn't take his eyes off of my chest. "That doesn't exactly look waterproof."

I pulled down the rest of my dress, tossing it to the side, revealing my black lace gartered thong. I strutted over to him tracing my fingers down his chest. It wasn't exactly the most comfortable thing I ever worn, with the form fitting boning in the torso, but I was hoping it would be off soon. I pursed my lips together and whispered in his ear. "Maybe you should see if it is." I moved his hand between my legs.

He just held his hand there for about five second before pulling away. "Libby." He held his hands up.

"Blaine." I breathed and put my arms around his neck. "Don't you want me?"

"I...I...I mean." He stuttered. He still couldn't take his eyes off of my chest.

"You mean what baby?" I said coyly, rubbing the lace garter on my thigh, on the bulge in his pants.

He sighed and closed his eyes pressing his forehead to mine. "I do Libby, I do. It's just..." He sighed.

"It's just what?" I retorted, pulling away and putting my hands on my hips. "You still want your ex? You think I'm ugly? You want my cousin?" I threw my hands up in the air. "For God's sake Blaine, what is it!"

He groaned and sat on the bed, putting his head in

his hands. "Libbyyyyyyy." He seemed to drag out the end of my name forever.

"Blaineeeeeeeee." I mocked back. I did not waste all of this money on perfectly good lingerie.

He patted the spot next to him on the bed. I reluctantly sat down, crossing my arms across my stomach.

He shook his head back and forth before turning and opening his eyes toward me. "Baby, you know I care about you."

"Then why..." He lifted up a hand as to say I'm not done.

"But..." He sighed loudly and over exaggerated. "I'm not just going to screw you in Jackson's bedroom." He put his arms around me and pulled me closer. "You are more than just some random skank that I'd hump and dump, and I hope you think more of yourself than that."

I didn't want to think of him humping or skanking anyone, and I kind of winced when he said that.

"Baby." He tilted my chin up toward him. "Do you really just want to have meaningless sex with me on Jackson's bed? Right this very moment?"

"Well." I bit my lip. "Not when you put it that way."

He groaned and not in the good way.

"Blaine, do you not understand how I'm feeling?" I moved my hands back and motioned them in a circle encompassing my torso. "I spent an entire paycheck on this. And not only that, but you have acted like doing anything more than kissing me is like some kind of a crime!"

"Libby. I do want to. Trust me." He ran his fingers

along the front of my panties, thumbing the lace in his fingertips. His very touch was proving that the panties were definitely not waterproof. "More than anything."

I leaned in closer and whispered. "Then why don't you?"

He moved his hand back up to my hip. "Because you mean too much to me to throw you down here on Jackson's bed!" He was almost yelling, I hoped no one heard him.

"Well fine. Why don't we go over to my place then, no one is going to be home all day." I scooted in closer so that I was practically on his lap, from the angle I was sitting and the rumbling in his pants, I could tell that I was making a pretty good argument.

He put his head down and whispered something I couldn't understand.

"What?"

"I can't Libby, I'm sorry." He didn't look up at me as he spoke.

"Why? It's obviously not like you have a problem in the keeping-it-up department." I nudged his bulge with my thigh.

He didn't move for a minute and then slowly pushed my thigh out of the way. "Look Libby." He stared me down. I couldn't tell what was behind his eyes or what he was thinking, and I wanted more than ever to know. "I'm not going to have sex with you here. End of story."

He took his arms out from around me and slowly stood up, adjusting himself as he did.

"Okay." I bit the inside of my cheek and then sprang up off of the bed, clasping my hands together.

"Well no one is at my Aunt Dee's right now, we can go there."

I positioned myself back in front of him, my body pressing tightly against his. "I'll even bring the bubblegum pink bedspread back out for you." I grabbed his hands and intertwined them with mine.

He groaned and made a circle with his neck before looking me straight in the eyes. I knew the look behind them now, and it was anger.

"Elizabeth." He growled. He had never called me Elizabeth before. He released his hands from mine and stomped toward the door.

"We are not having this conversation anymore. It's done." He put his hand on the door and took a deep breath. "Now come on, people are going to wonder where we have been."

I crossed my arms over my chest and just stood there. I was in shock and had no idea what to say. So I mumbled the only thing I could think of. "No."

"What was that?" He tilted his head so that his left ear was closer to me.

"I said no, Blaine." I said a little louder. "Isn't that what you just said to me over and over?" I smirked and grabbed my dress.

"Come on Libby, it doesn't have to be like that, let's just go back outside get a few beers and have a good time." He forced a tight lipped smile.

"No, Blaine." I slipped the dress over my head. "Take me home."

He sighed and walked over to me, putting his hands on my shoulders as I pulled the rest of my dress down. "Baby can't we just wait a bit longer? Not just have it be some meaningless sex in Jackson's bed? Or trying to sneak behind your Aunt to do it in your bedroom?" He eyes looked at me, pleading like puppy dogs.

"So is all sex going to be meaningless with me?" I pushed back. "Or just when you don't want it?"

"Libby..."

"No Blaine." I balled my hands into tiny fists and tightly crossed my arms across my chest.

"Take me home."

"Libby. Come on." He pleaded again, trying to make eye contact with me.

I looked down at the ground, grinding my feet into the wooden plank floor. "Please just take me home."

With a sigh he agreed and I spent the rest of the night, by myself, on the bathroom floor. My cheeks were soaked with tears and the toilet was a swirling mass of lemon shake up and cookie dough. I laid my head down on the cold tile floor until I heard Aunt Dee unlock the front door. Then I quickly washed my face and headed to bed.

I had never felt so rejected in my life, even Beau wanted me, but my own boyfriend wouldn't even sleep with me when I was right on top of him, in black lingerie that cost hundreds of dollars.

Blaine called, texted, and Facebook messaged me dozens of times that night, but I ignored every single one of them. All of the I'm sorries and please talk to me's. And one point he even showed up at Aunt Dee's house, but I couldn't bear to see him. I was embarrassed, but more than that I was hurt, and it was going to take a lot for me to get over that.

CHAPTER 16

I missed Blaine. I was still ignoring his texts and calls. When he would come into work I would make some excuse so that I could go to the backroom and sort through whatever junk people had brought in. My heart was already paper-thin and now it was starting to rip.

People at work were starting to notice something was going on. I wasn't eating and if I was eating, I was running straight back to the bathroom. I was always tired and started keeping to myself more. I knew Aunt Dee was worried about me, but of all people I never thought she would ask Dina to talk to me.

I could hear her gum chomping, getting louder and louder as she approached my desk. "Um, Libby?"

I didn't even look up from my computer. "Yeah Dina?"

"Um yeah, like can we talk?" Chomp, chomp.

"We are talking Dina." I sighed.

"No." She pouted. "I mean like go for a walk or something, alone, get out of here?"

"Dina." I stared blankly at the computer screen. I had been staring at blank excel document for the past hour. "I'm working."

"Please?" She begged in her semi-nasally, whiny

voice.

I took a deep breath and turned away from my computer. "Fine." I stood up. "I will go for a damn walk with you."

I locked my eyes on Dina, looking her up and down. How could Blaine sleep with her and not me? She was skinnier than me. Her boney shoulders looked like baby chicken wings sticking out of the top of her shirt. Or maybe he just preferred brunettes, like Julie, but Dina's hair was more of a, dirty bottom of the sink, brown. Whatever it was, it was bothering me. I concentrated on looking at the ground instead as we walked out the front door of the office.

"I noticed Blaine hasn't been around lately." She piped up as we started down the sidewalk.

"Yeah, so? Now you don't have anything good to look at in the shop besides old pottery?" I kept my eyes down, but I couldn't keep my sarcasm in check. "Or maybe you just want to tell me some more about how you screwed my boyfriend. Oh, wait no it was before he met me, so it's okay right?" My voice was getting louder as I tried to hold back tears.

"Maybe Blaine just doesn't want to be with me? Maybe I'm not good enough, just another college flunky. Another blonde sorority bimbo he can just toss to the side." I could feel the tears that were streaming my cheeks, stinging my eyes. I wiped them with the back of my hand and plopped down on a bench, putting my head between my knees.

Dina took a deep, long breath and just stared down at me for a minute, her ugly black loafers tapping against the pavement.

She slowly sat down beside me and put her hands

on her knees. "Libby, I honestly don't think that's it at all."

"Then what?" I practically spit, putting my face in my hands. "I just don't know what to do anymore. I can't even face him."

She took another deep long breath. "Let's face it Libby, you and I aren't really friends."

"No shit." I sniffled.

"Anyway." She leaned back. "My point is that there is a lot you don't know about me and a lot that you probably should."

I had no idea what this had to do with me and Blaine, but she continued anyways.

"Well, I bet you didn't know I used to date Jackson?"

I looked up at her raising an eyebrow. She didn't look at me, just straight ahead. Turns out Dina isn't in her thirties, she was only 24. You think I would know that from writing her paychecks, but like I said, I was terrible at math.

"Well, Jackson and I did date for a long time. I thought we were going to get married. I moved back here after finishing school at Tulane, started here doing appraisals, and immediately started dating Jackson."

Her expression never changed. She just stared off into space like she was going into another world.

"Now Blaine and Jackson started working together the summer after Blaine graduated high school, and they quickly became friends. I remember that first summer, he and Julie were always over."

I shuddered as she said Julie's name, but Dina didn't notice. She was still just staring straight ahead.

"He lost his virginity to her that summer, you know?"

I actually had no idea. Julie was something Blaine and I cared not to discuss. I just knew that there had been a lot of girls, but I didn't know that Julie was the first. But I couldn't speak at that moment, it was like my mouth had swelled up, so I just shook my head.

"That's why he was so crushed when she broke up with him. He saved it all those years for her. And that little wench held it over his head for years. Then finally the night before she left for college they finally did it, right there on Jackson's bed."

Well I guess that made sense why he wouldn't have sex with me at Jackson's...

"Do you know how many times I washed those sheets?" She wrinkled her nose. I couldn't help but laugh. "Girl was nasty!"

I laughed again, a real laugh, one that I hadn't had since the Fourth of July.

"Well it's obvious why he was so crushed when she broke up with him. For weeks he just tried nothing but to get her back. Calling her all the time, trying to plan trips up to Mississippi, but she just wasn't interested."

Dina tugged her skirt down a bit, and then glanced at me to make sure I was still paying attention. I nodded to show that I was.

"About a month later he found out that she had a new boyfriend. Some fraternity boy at Ole Miss, Beta or Gamma or something or another. Anyway Blaine was completely mortified. He didn't know which way was up."

An elderly lady walked past us to go to the post

office and we sat in silence giving a polite smile as she passed. Dina watched her until she walked into the post office and then closed the door.

Dina took a deep breath and then stared down at the sidewalk below us.

"Well that night he found out about Julie, Jackson decided to have a little 'forget about Julie' party. He got some beers and some pot and everyone was having a pretty good time."

Dina tugged on her skirt again. It was kind of, her nervous tick.

"Let me put it this way, Blaine was having a really good time. He was definitely three sheets to the wind. I don't even know how he was walking."

I wasn't too sure where this story was going, but I knew a drunk and high Blaine was probably not a good thing.

"And you know Blaine has always been one of the most attractive guys in the Parrish. I mean star pitcher in high school and those blue eyes, they are what girls have dreams about."

How I missed his blue eyes.

"Well it wasn't just Blaine that was a little smashed, it was all of us...and well Jackson and I had a big fight."

Then I knew exactly where this was going.

"I was the first in Blaine's series of random girls, and right there on the bed that Jackson and I had shared so many moments."

She looked right at me, her beady little black eyes welding back tears. "Jackson was going to propose to me that night. I couldn't find him because he was planning the perfect proposal out by the boat dock.

And when I didn't show he came looking for me and he found me alright."

She took a big sniffle, looking back down at the ground.

"Blaine was practically passed out on the bed, so naturally it was all my fault. He came into that room and there I was naked as the day I was born laying next to Blaine on his bed."

She started tapping her feet on the ground.

"He threw the ring box at me." She looked back at me. "It was a beautiful ring, more than I think he actually could afford. He must have saved for months."

She looked back down. "But it ended that night and as for Blaine. Well." She snorted. "He didn't even remember it. When I tried to talk to him the next day, you know thinking we could go to the Tasty Freeze or something, he acted like I was dirt or something."

She shook her head.

"But that didn't stop him from moving on to the next girl and the next girl. It was like he thought he could drown his sorrows in alcohol and vagina."

"Wow." It was all I could scratch out. My throat was so dry from my tears.

"But that's not the point of the story, Libby." She looked at me again. It was like those beady black eyes were pleading with me.

"Then what is it Dina? Why should I care so much for a guy that doesn't care about me?" A single tear rolled down my cheek and I left it there.

"Libby, he has never looked at another girl like he looks at you, not even Julie. Hell if it wasn't for you, I think he would have probably screwed the whole town!"

I snorted. That was probably true, and he probably would again now that he was done with me.

"Libby." Dina's expression was sober. "He didn't have sex with you at Jackson's because he wasn't going to have you just be another random girl, or even worse have you leave him like Julie did. Don't you see that?"

"I don't know, don't you think that's a bit of a stretch?" I bit my lip, trying to avoid her eyes.

"Honey, I don't think you understand. If you would have seen how he was before you, you wouldn't be saying this." She gave up trying to look me in the eye and just shook her head.

Then we sat there quietly for a few moments before she stood up. "I'm only going to say one more thing to you, Libby."

I looked up at her, her cheeks were actually soaking wet. "If I could have one more chance with Jackson I would take it in a heartbeat, and I think you should do the same with Blaine."

She didn't wait for me to follow, just left me there staring up as she darted back down the street and into the antique shop.

CHAPTER 17

I just stared at my phone for a long time, debating if I should pick it up and call him or not.

"Libby just call him!" Britt yelled from the other end of the couch.

It was Thursday, which meant it was bridge night. Since it was Eleanor Saint Fleur's night to host, it was just Britt and I sitting on the couch and watching a made-for-TV movie.

"That's not what I'm thinking about," I quipped, quickly looking up at the TV.

Britt rolled her eyes. "Libby, I'm not stupid, it's been almost a week since you talked to him, and I know you want to. So just call him!"

"I don't need to call him. I'm enjoying sitting here with you and watching this movie." I slouched deeper into the couch.

"What's this movie about then?"

"What?" I shot my head toward her.

"You heard me. If you are watching this movie, what is it about?" She raised her eyebrows.

"Uh...well...there is a lady...and a dude..."

"Just as I thought." Britt leaned across the couch and grabbed my phone.

"Hey!" I reached my arms out, but it was too late. Britt had already sprung up and was behind the couch. The phone was to her ear.

"Hey Blaine, its Britt." I hopped over the couch mouthing No over and over and waving my arms in the air. "Yeah, I've got someone that wants to talk to you."

She handed me the phone. "I'm going to Sarah's, I'll be back later, now don't keep that boy waiting." She then turned and headed out the front door, leaving me standing there with the phone in my hand.

"Um hello? Hello?" I could hear Blaine loud and clear.

Slowly I put the phone up to my ear. "Hey..."

"Libby, is it really you this time?" He spoke slowly, really bringing out his accent.

"Yeah...it's me..." I couldn't think of anything to say. I didn't know what I was supposed to say, so we just sat there in silence for what seemed like forever.

"Libby, I'm sorry." It was all he could muster. It felt like he was fighting the words as he said them.

"Are you?" I held back my tears, they really wanted to come out though, and I constantly had to wipe my eyes.

Then the doorbell rang. I quickly wiped my eyes again. "Hold on, someone's at the door."

I walked over, taking a big sniffle, with the phone still at my ear.

"Yes?" I dropped the phone as soon as I saw that it was Blaine standing there. His eyes were blood shot, like he hadn't slept in days, and he looked like he just picked up whatever wrinkled flannel shirt and jeans he could find on the floor.

"Baby, I'm so sorry." He just stood there, looking right at me, his eyes were so blue and I realized how much I missed his stare.

I completely lost it. I let the tears run freely as I jumped into his arms, almost knocking him over. Luckily he caught me and I wrapped my legs and arms around him.

He looked up at me, gripping me tighter around the waist and a big smile crossed his face. I looked down and finally met his smile, and then I leaned in closer and lightly kissed his lips.

He reciprocated in full force, opening his mouth and kissing me hard as he walked into the house, with me still in his arms. Luckily he found the couch. I was afraid he might lose his balance.

He stopped kissing me for a brief moment, but then started up again as he laid down on top of me on the couch. It was like he had never kissed me or felt me before, his hands were running through my hair, then up my sides, and down to my hips. Then his kissing got harder and he started going down my neck and my collar bone.

"Blaine, what are you doing?" I pulled his head up and looked at him.

"What?" He shrugged, intertwining his fingers with the drawstring on my sweat pants.

"You act like you haven't seen me in years or like that you want something." I cocked my head to the side.

"Well, it has been awhile, baby." He grinned from ear to ear. "And I missed you." He leaned in again to kiss me, but I turned my head sharply before he could, giving him a mouthful of blonde hair.

"This doesn't mean I've completely forgiven you, or that I'm just going to have sex with you here on Aunt

Dee's couch." I slowly turned my head back toward him so he could see that I was serious.

"Well isn't that what you want, Libby?" He moved from the drawstring to the top of my sweat pants. He moved my shirt up and rubbed my panty line with his thumb.

"I do...I mean..." I pushed his hand away and moved my legs out from around him and onto the floor. "I mean, I did." I put my head in my hands and heaved a big sigh.

"So, you don't want to now?" He scooted closer to me, a look of puzzlement clearly painted on his face. "Did I do something to change your mind? Baby, I am truly very sorry what happened on the fourth, and I really want to make it up to you."

He gently grabbed my hand, putting it in his.

I looked up at him, slowly pulling my head up. "I know Blaine, and I know I should have been more understanding of everything. I shouldn't have kept trying to force you."

"Baby, you didn't try to force me into anything. I was just being stupid and stubborn." He smiled scooting closer to me. "And I am really hoping that you still have that little black thing you were wearing."

I grinned and shook my head. "I think I buried that somewhere in my closet."

"Damn." The air blew threw his nose as he laughed.

"I do have some pretty awesome granny panties on right now though."

"Man, Libby." He poked my ribs. "You really know how to get a guy going."

"You know what would really get me going?" I

turned my whole body toward him, a devious little grin crossing my lips.

"What?" He was so close I could feel that he was still a bit excited, well at least his pants were telling me he was still excited.

I leaned in and put my lips close to his ear, whispering. "If you got me a root beer float."

"Oh come on!" He smacked his leg.

"What?" I pulled back. "We haven't gone to Sam's in a while now, and I really want one."

"You're a tease." He poked the bit of my stomach that peeked out from underneath my shirt. "And you look like you need to eat."

"I don't know how I'm supposed to take that one, do I thank you?"

"Um no." He stood up. "It means you need to eat a fucking cheeseburger."

I frowned and crossed my arms over my chest. "Well, that wasn't very nice."

He groaned. "Libby, c'mon I don't want to play this game. Let's go. I'll take you to Sam's or the Tasty Freeze." He put his hand out toward me.

I smacked his hand down. "I don't want to go now."

"What did I do now? I just said that you were skinny. Is that such a bad thing?" He threw his arms up in the air in disarray.

"No, I guess it isn't." I stood up and grabbed his hand. "Fine, you can take me to Sam's."

I wished that I could tell Blaine. I wished that I could just open up to him, tell him Why yes Blaine, I look so skinny because I've thrown up everything I've eaten since we fought. Or how I never thought I was fat till college.

Sororities are notorious for hazing, that's no secret. They say it's more regulated, but the truth is it still happens a lot. It's really not all bad, it shows you know that the older members have earned this and they do deserve respect. So I really didn't mind the study hours and house clean up, but what I did mind was the bikini test.

I thought the bikini test was just a rumor, something that they made up during rush week so girls wouldn't want to join a sorority. I was definitely wrong. The first night I was a new pledge, they had all the new girls line up and then strip down to just our bra and panties. We all thought this was weird, but at the same time, we still had the adrenaline from rush pumping in our veins.

All of a sudden the Alpha Mu boys came down the cement stairs, to the unfinished Kappa basement, all holding Sharpies, and quickly each of them picked a girl and started circling their trouble spots. Lots of girls had circles all over their stomachs and the like. I looked around at all of them and was just shocked at what I was seeing.

Finally, Beau came up to me. He was the lucky one that got to Sharpie me. I thought he might say something sweet, maybe not even Sharpie me, but I couldn't be that lucky.

"Well, I mean, you are pretty fine." He slowly stepped in front of me and then circled around me, ever so slowly, like he was a vulture and I was his prey.

"I mean tall and blonde does have its advantages, but..."

I snapped my head foreword, but?

He took the Sharpie and made the two biggest circles on each of my thighs. "You've got some of the biggest thunder thighs I have ever seen!"

Everyone in the room laughed. The new recruits tried to hold back their giggles, but I think most of them were just relieved it wasn't them. Beau never apologized for that. To this day I don't think he realized how much it affected me.

I couldn't stop eating, I really liked food, but I also found out if you binged it was just as easy to purge. It took me a while to get the knack of it. Sometimes I wouldn't be able to throw up at all, and would just feel sick. Then I started using whatever object I could: straws, spoons, whatever. Soon it was like I could throw up on demand. I would just go in the bathroom, run the water, and come out about five minutes later. My eyes would be a little bloodshot and my knees a little red from the floor.

I was beginning to be happy with who I'd become after moving to Louisiana, but with Blaine's rejection I felt like I was back in the basement in the Kappa house. But this time it was Blaine with the Sharpie.

CHAPTER 18

The next day at work it was like nothing had changed. Blaine came to get me as usual for lunch and we spent our nights watching movies on the couch at Aunt Dee's. But Saturday was a little out of the ordinary.

My phone vibrated loudly on the dresser, waking me up.

One New Message from Blaine

I unlocked my phone and read the message

Blaine:
Happy One month anniversary. I know it's cheesy, but I'll see you later ☺

I smiled. A guy who actually remembered something silly like a one month anniversary. I don't even think Beau remembered the night we met.

I texted back.

Can't wait! ☺

∞

I had no idea what Blaine and I were doing. It was only a month that we were official, and he asked me out on the picnic table at the Tasty Freeze so it's not like I was expecting roses and jewelry. Though he did seem to always notice my bits of jewelry from Tiffany's that I would wear, and would comment on them. But I knew that definitely wasn't coming my way. I wasn't sure how much Blaine made working for the Parrish Highway and Roads Department, but I knew he had to be putting away some money, since he was living at home.

Most of the morning and afternoon nothing really happened. I kept trying to text Blaine, but he said he was busy. I had no idea what he could be doing. Hopefully he was planning something awesome for that night.

But as the day pegged on, I had almost watched an entire season of some mindless reality TV show and was afraid I'd be doing that for the rest of the night.

"Libby, can you move your laundry hamper out of the way?"

I was sprawled out on the couch, when I heard Aunt Dee pummeling into the kitchen.

"What?" I sat up and saw Aunt Dee carrying a big plastic box from my bedroom and putting it on the kitchen table. "What are you doing Aunt Dee?"

"Oh." She stopped and looked up at me. "Well, the ladies and I are going to be having a scrapbooking night here, since Britt will be out and you'll be over at The Crabtree's."

"What?" I stood up and walked toward the kitchen while Aunt Dee went into my room and quickly brought out another big box of scrapbooking supplies.

"Well honey, I haven't scrapbooked since you've

gotten here and a lot has happened!" She put her tiny hands on her hips and looked up at me.

"No, that's fine I'm not questioning that." I ran my fingers through my hair. "You just said I was going to the Crabtree's?"

"Well that's what Vicki had told me when she called this morning. She said Blaine's got something planned for him and Libby, so let's have a scrapbooking night. You didn't know?" She pushed up her glasses.

"Oh yeah, knew all about it. Um what time did he say he was picking me up again?" I took a big stretch, putting my arms over my head so I towered even more over her.

"Well the girls are supposed to be over here at six for the potluck, so hopefully soon." She scampered back into the bedroom, pulling out more boxes. The lady had a lot of scrapbooking supplies.

I glanced over at the microwave clock. It was quarter to five. I figured Blaine would be over in an hour. The boy was usually early, which meant that I didn't have much time. I knew if he was planning something I'd have to come up with the perfect gift for him, and I had a pretty good idea what that could be. I ran into the bedroom and jumped on my laptop as fast as I could. Only an hour to get this ordered, shower, change, and do my hair. It was going to be a rush.

∞

At six o'clock on the dot, women with giant scrapbooking bags piled in through the door. They dragged their bags with one hand and carried either a crock-pot or some other dish in their other hand. Britt was already gone, camping with Sarah or something for the weekend, so that left me to help everyone in.

It took me literally only forty-five minutes to shower, do my hair, makeup, and get dressed. A record if I do say so myself, but Blaine wasn't there. He was never late and I was starting to get a little worried.

At 6:15 Blaine's mom, Vicki, finally showed up.

"Hey Libby." She was breathing heavy as she lugged her big scrapbooking case in one hand and handed me a Tupperware container with the other.

"Hey, Mrs. Crabtree." I set the Tupperware container down as she went to the table that was set up in the living room. Aunt Dee made me help her push the couch and love seat to the sides so she could have a big enough table for everyone to work at.

"Yes dear?" She started pulling things out of her bag and putting them onto the table.

"Um, is Blaine supposed to be picking me up, or did he have to go run an errand or something?" I twirled a stray strand of hair nervously and rapidly.

I never knew what to wear, or to do with my hair around Blaine. I could dress up and he would surprise me by wearing jeans and a t-shirt and take me to the bowling alley. Or I would throw on whatever was handy and he would plan on taking me to dinner in New Orleans. It was never a winning situation with me.

So I tried to stick with a middle ground: white capris, a pink cami, and a purple short sleeve shrug. I decided to go against the heels, since they seemed to get me in trouble, and stuck with some purple flats and just let my hair fall loosely around my shoulders. It wasn't like the humidity would let me do anything more with it anyways. If the Kappa girls could see me now, they would never believe I would go this long without a straightener.

"Oh." Mrs. Crabtree looked me over. "Well he should have been here by now. That boy has been busy all day."

"Really now?" I leaned in with a smile crossing my lips.

"Oh honey, I've never seen him as crazy as he's been today, wanting to get us all out of the house." She rustled through her scrapbooking supplies.

"Hmmm....do you know what he's planning?" I laid my hands on the fold out chair that her stuff was sitting on.

"She won't be telling you anything, if she knows what's good for her." Blaine put his arms around me, chiming in. I didn't even hear him come in.

"Why Blaine, I wasn't going to tell her nothing!" His mom waved her hand in the air before letting it fall flat.

"Sure you weren't, Ma. I know you too well." He looked down at me. "You ready?"

I wasn't too sure what to expect and what he would be dressed in. Since he was in his usual shorts and a t-shirt, I figured it wasn't going to be anything too fancy.

I turned toward him. "Well look who finally showed up?" I released his arms from around me and put my hands on my hips.

"Libby." He tilted his head back and his eyes met

mine. "When you get to my house I can explain everything."

"Fine." I let out a deep breath and then turned back to the ladies. "Bye everyone, see you later."

They didn't even seem to notice we were leaving. They were too busy setting up their food and supplies.

"So what did you spend all day doing?" I asked as Blaine got into the driver's seat.

"Well, that's the complicated thing." Blaine said as he started up the car. "You know how I make fun of you for not being able to cook? Well it turns out I'm even worse!"

I laughed. "Do tell."

He started out of Aunt Dee's driveway and down the road. "I was trying to make homemade pralines, you know southern candy?"

He glanced at me and I nodded to show that I was paying attention.

"Well I guess when it's humid, that doesn't really work too well. I ended up just causing a small fire in the kitchen."

"You caught your kitchen on fire?" I covered my mouth to try and hide my laughter.

"Well not a big fire." His cheeks flushed.

"I'm sorry." I put my hand on his knee and grabbed his hand, intertwining our fingers.

It always amazed me how perfect our hands fit into each other's. I always felt like my hands were abnormally long and looked like that of an alien. But his thick, tanned hands, always rough from working outside and not using lotion, like I begged, they almost made my hands look tiny.

We pulled up to his house just as a slow country song finished on the radio. It was funny how I never really paid attention to country. I actually always held something against it when I was back home. But after moving to Louisiana and meeting Blaine, country music had a whole new meaning. I could find a song, by the same artist mind you, to be able to listen to when I was depressed, overjoyed, or just in the mood to dance. I would never admit it to anyone here, but I was actually enjoying the slow beat of the country music.

Blaine came around the other side of the car and opened my door as he always did. But instead of letting me get out on my own he scooped me up out of the car and took me in his arms, carrying me like a fireman would.

"Blaine Crabtree, what do you think you are doing?"

He grinned and closed the door to his truck with his back before walking toward the house.

"What? Haven't you ever had a guy sweep you off your feet before?"

"Would that require a broom or something?" I giggled.

"Nope." He stepped up the porch steps and let me down as soon as we got in the foyer. "But I think I made a pretty good effort without it."

"I think I was thoroughly swept." I tipped up a bit on my toes and pressed my lips to his.

He returned the favor pressing against me and slowly wrapped his arms tight around my waist. I moved my arms around his neck when he stopped.

"What?" I pouted out my bottom lip.

He grinned and moved my arms from around his neck. "Just hold on one second, I have something for you." He raised one finger and then darted out down the hallway.

I shook my head and kneeled down, digging into my purse.

"Do you ever leave that purse alone?" He quipped when he came back into the room with his hands behind his back.

"Blaine." I stood up, holding an envelope behind my back. "This is not just a purse, it's Prada."

He rolled his eyes. "Anyway."

He removed his hands from behind his back and in his hands was a small box about the size of a dictionary, crudely wrapped in the day's newspaper.

"Gee." I grimaced taking the box.

"Well, open it!" He motioned his hands up.

I slowly ripped the newspaper off, which was almost too slow for Blaine. His eyebrows were completely raised as his eyes followed my hands.

"Um, cigars?" I held up the box. It was a white box with some Spanish writing on it. My dad used to get imported cigars from a client, so I recognized the boxes.

"Libby, would I really buy you cigars?"

I raised an eyebrow.

He let out a big sigh. "No, I wouldn't."

He made an opening motion with his hands. "It's what's inside of the box."

I stopped holding the box up, and sat it up, slowly opening it. Inside was an old, completely full, pack of Dijarum Blacks, or cloves. The ones that Blaine smoked and I hated. I wrinkled my nose.

"Um, you know I don't like cloves."

"Exactly!" He clasped his hands together. "Which is why I'm giving you my last pack."

"Um?" I held the pack up raising an eyebrow.

"Baby, I know you're blonde."

He ran a hand through his hair.

"It means that I haven't smoked in a week." He came in closer and put his arms around my waist. "And it means since you don't like them, I'm quitting."

"Really?" My look of confusing turned into actual joy.

There were a lot of things I hated that Beau did. Constant drinking with his fraternity buddies, smoking pot, calling girls 'bitches', and there were a lot more. But any time I asked him to stop any of these things, he just laughed at me and said I was cute. It was the first time a guy actually listened to what I had to say and heeded my advice. It was actually the first time anyone had really quit doing something when I asked them. It actually meant a lot more than I think Blaine even realized. Suddenly I felt like I was the one with the Sharpie this time.

He leaned in closing his eyes to kiss me again, but I turned my head. "Wait."

"What now?" He groaned.

"No, nothing bad." I pulled out the envelope that I had behind me and held it between us.

"What's this?" He took the envelope from my hand and stepped back a bit.

"Well, you have to open it!" I mocked.

He grinned and shook his head, ripping open the envelope as he did.

"A plane ticket?"

I stepped in closer. "I want you to know that just because I am going to Kristi's wedding doesn't mean I am leaving Louisiana, or you."

I tugged on his belt loop pulling him closer. "Kristi's wedding is next month, and I know I asked you to go with me, but I want you to know that I really do want you to go with me."

He stopped looking at the ticket and met my gaze.

"I'm not ashamed of you or anything about Elsbury. I want to show you off as my amazingly sexy Louisiana man."

He smiled and leaned in pressing his lips to mine again. He held me there for a while, his tongue dancing behind my lips, until we were interrupted, as usual, by his phone vibrating his pants pocket.

He groaned. "Hold that thought baby."

He picked up the phone and walked into the living room, putting the plane ticket on an end table as he went.

I really wanted to snoop around to see what he had planned. I could still smell burnt sugar and pecans wafting in from the kitchen. The dogs were out on the porch snoring away, and everything else just seemed perfectly normal. I had no idea what else he could have planned.

He stepped back in the room sliding his phone back in his pocket. "Sorry, the guys were hoping we'd meet them out at the pool hall."

"Oh." I looked down, thinking that a romantic evening was definitely not happening.

"But." He came closer and lifted my chin up, planting a kiss on my forehead. "I told them I was busy, about to kick your ass at Duck Hunt." He grinned letting go of me and starting up the stairs.

"Wait, you have the original Nintendo?" I had to run to follow him up the stairs.

"Well yeah, it's the only way to go!" He called as I was almost a full flight behind him. "It's up in my room. Come on, I don't have all night!"

I practically flew up the stairs to see him standing in the doorway of his room. But it wasn't a TV set up with a Nintendo. Almost the exact opposite. The room was entirely lit by dozens of candles (the LED ones, he didn't want to start another fire). He had changed his sheets and bedspread so it was no longer a big flannel mess, but a black feather down comforter and six pillows sitting at the head of the bed. All that was missing was wine and music, I thought. It was cheesy and romantic and nerve racking all at the same time.

I covered my mouth, trying to stifle a giggle.

"What?" He put his arms out. "Too much?"

"It is a little cheesy." I giggled, removing my hand from my mouth.

"Dangit." He shook his head walking back up toward me. "I just wanted to do something...to make it you know...special and what not."

I bit my lip looking down at the floor. "Are you sure?"

"Libby." He lifted my chin up so my eyes met his. "I'm not going to do anything you don't want to do."

He took my hand and led me further into the room.

"When I wouldn't sleep with you at Jackson's, it wasn't because I didn't want to. Trust me, I did." He grinned blowing the air out of his nose.

"I just wasn't going to have it be some meaningless

thing, just throwing you down on someone else's waterbed at a party. You are definitely too good for that, and I wanted to make sure that is not how you remembered the first time we did it."

I had wished that Beau would have said something like that. It was no secret that I lost my virginity to Beau, a week after I had met him, and even before the Sharpie incident. I was very drunk and practically passed out on his bed. He didn't care that his sheets hadn't been washed since spring break, or that the whole thing was only about two minutes long. But somehow I knew it wouldn't be like that with Blaine.

He stepped in even closer and slowly pulled his shirt off throwing it to the side. I was definitely not disappointed as I ran my fingers across the tattoo below his left shoulder blade and above his chest.

"Joie De Vivre?" I questioned, putting another arm around his torso.

"Zhwah duh viv-re" He said in a French accent. "It means the joy of living."

I looked up at him. "Then let's enjoy." I leaned in closer and kissed him hard on the mouth.

He pulled me closer, pressing his body against mine while his tongue made his way between my lips. I wrapped my arms tightly around his neck while he ran his hands through my hair and let them trail down my shoulders and lower back. I actually cursed under my breath that I didn't wear the black lingerie, and he laughed at that saying there would be another time for that.

It didn't start out as the most romantic thing ever, but I don't think it's ever like the movies. I was very nervous and kept shaking as he slowly pulled off my shrug and cami. For a moment he just stared, tracing his fingers underneath my bra line.

"You know baby, we don't have to do anything you don't want to do." He leaned in and placed featherlike kisses along my collarbone before looking back up at me. "We can still play Duck Hunt…"

I tugged on his belt loops pulling him closer. I could already feel him beneath his pants. He removed my bra slowly as he brushed up against my skin. It was like he was trying to remember every curve.

Not everything can be perfect though, when you try and walk and remove pants, there is a lot of stumbling involved. Finally we reached the bed while Blaine practically fell on top of me as he kicked out of his pants. He reached down and slid off my capris and panties, kissing all the way down my legs. Slowly he started to peel off his boxers when I reached a hand up and pressed it against the top of his underwear line.

"Wait," I whispered.

"Do you really want to stop right now?" He looked down at me with pleading eyes. He had already pitched a tent and was practically falling out. And with his size it looked like that was not an easy task to keep in.

"No." I bit my lip. "But…um do you…you know have something? You know a wrap it before you tap it?" I was naked on my boyfriend's bed, yet still couldn't say the word.

He smiled brightly. "You mean a condom, Libby?"

"Yeah." I could feel the blood rise up in my cheeks.

He just smiled not saying a word, and leaned over to his night stand, pulling out a golden wrapped condom. Slowly he slid off his boxers and tossed them to the floor. Then he opened the wrapper, but stopped before putting it on.

"Do you want to do it?" He held the condom up.

"Ew!" I scrunched my face.

"Really Libby?" He cocked an eyebrow.

I sighed. "Blaine, please just do me already."

He took it slow, none of the high paced two pump chump that Beau was notorious for. Even though I wasn't that experienced, I would have to say he was really good. He actually cared about me finishing more than himself. Whispering over and over you're beautiful. Even up until the moment we both reached the climactic end, his eyes never left mine.

We just laid there for awhile, him on his back, and me with my head on his chest and his hand running through my hair.

"I hope that was better than it would have been in Jackson's waterbed." He smiled, looking down at me.

"Hmmm." I propped myself up onto my stomach, still lying on his chest. "Let's see, us alone in your house on satin sheets." I traced my fingers down his abs. "Or on Jackson's Spiderman sheets, with probably half the Parrish listening in on us."

"I know." He took in a big sarcastic sigh. "Tough call."

I smiled and leaned in and kissed him again, which if there are two people naked in bed together, a kiss always leads to something more. Which it did. Twice.

CHAPTER 19

Once Blaine and I started, it was like it never ended. Soon we couldn't get enough of each other. And once we got the romantic sex out of the way it seemed like it was okay to do it anywhere. On our lunch hour, running to his parent's, in his truck, in the stairwell. The one place I refused to do it was outside. There were a lot of animals in the swamp.

"Come on, it's not like something is going to come out of the swamp and attack us." He would beg.

"But it could." I would argue.

And that would be the end of it, and we would have to drive like hell to get to his house to have a quickie, before our lunch break was over.

Since Blaine had fully committed to going to Kristi's wedding, I convinced him that he had to get a new suit. After a lot of pleading, on my part, and whining, on his part, I finally convinced him to drive to New Orleans on a Saturday and go suit shopping.

"So this means I get two blow jobs at my beck and call, one time of sex whenever and wherever, and you have to cook me dinner." He counted off on his hand as we drove down the highway to New Orleans.

"Except." I put down his fingers, leaning over the seat of his truck. "No outside sex and dinner can be from a box."

He exhaled deeply. "Okay, but you have to make dessert then!"

I leaned in and kissed his cheek. "Deal."

I would have loved to take him to a tailor and to get a nice suit made, but that definitely wasn't Blaine's thing. In fact the nicest outfit Blaine even owned was the one he wore on our first date, and he confessed that was his usual funeral or wedding outfit. I didn't think that was going to fly in the Chicago suburbs.

Blaine grew up knowing most of his graduating class, about one hundred of them, but since I wasn't an athlete or a popular girl, I just seemed to fade into the crowd. Another big part of that was the fact that my graduating class had over one thousand students. Blaine didn't seem to understand that concept, or how my high school was bigger than the size of the whole town of Elsbury. This made me a little weary of taking him back home, not only was I from a large suburb, but also a rich one. In fact, my Prada bag, a graduation gift, some girls in my class received new cars, so my bag looked minimal.

But at least I didn't keep many of my friends from high school. There wasn't really too many anyways, a few girls I talked to in band, but once I went to college it was like a fresh start. I wasn't Big Bird anymore, I was actually noticed in a crowd, and it wasn't just for my height.

So at last, after Blaine gave in, and driving around for what seemed like hours, we ended up finding a mall in New Orleans. We decided to just head into a department store to find him a suit off of the rack.

"Can I get an orange suit?" He looked at me with pleading eyes while we walked hand in hand through the store.

"Well if my dress is yellow, don't you think that will clash?" I squeezed his hand.

"So we'll look like a 1970's patio set. I don't see the problem." He laughed.

Finally we made it over to the men's suits, where an overly flamboyant, short man with black spiky hair and a purple button-down shirt greeted us.

"Hey y'all, is there anything I can help you with?" He practically pranced over to us, clasping his hands.

"OH MY GOD!" He put his hands on the side of his face.

Blaine and I looked around to see what was wrong.

The salesman then pointed at my bag. "Is that a real Prada bag?"

"Um." I bit my lip looking down at the bag. Blaine covered his mouth trying to keep from laughing. Now if there was one thing I knew about Blaine, it was that even though he was a southern gentleman who liked to open doors and cared about if I climaxed, he was all in all a road worker, a man's man. Needless to say, he was not pleased with our salesman's love of my purse.

"Yeah, it is." I looked up at the clerk, who then turned his attention back to Blaine.

"Oh honey, you bagged yourself a good one here!" He practically squealed.

"Um, yeah." He put his arm around me flexing as he did to basically say, Yes I'm straight and I work for the road crew, me big, scary man grrr.

"Well now, what can I do for you two today? Do you need any help with anything? I am at your service." He curtsied.

"You see, Mister—" I squinted looking at his name tag. "Robbie." I let go of Blaine's hand and pointed both hands toward him. "My boyfriend here, Blaine, really needs a new suit for my sorority sister's wedding in August."

"Hmm." Robbie circled Blaine, tapping his fingers on his chin.

Blaine looked down at me with pleading eyes. I let go of his hand and edged him toward Robbie.

"It's in the Chicago suburbs." I continued. "They'll be getting married on a beach at a resort up in Chicago. My dress is a butter cream color, so make my man look pretty!" I patted Blaine on the back.

Blaine glanced back at me and mouthed, you owe me.

I laughed as Robbie took him by the arm. "I think I know just what we are going to do with you. Now come with me."

I tried to cover my giggles as Robbie pulled Blaine over to a big three-way mirror and started measuring him. Blaine especially got nervous when Robbie had to measure his inseam.

But Blaine was a good sport through it all, and took all my laughs and Robbie constantly walking into the dressing room to hand him clothes... no matter if Blaine was decent or not.

Finally after trying on about thirty different outfits, Blaine strolled out of the dressing room in a plain black suit. He wasn't exactly smiling when he came out, but I didn't think he could have looked any better. Robbie paired the suit with a plain white shirt and a tie that almost matched the color of the bridesmaid dress. Don't ask me how Robbie was able to match it so perfectly.

The suit fit Blaine in all of the right places, nothing tight or loose, he looked so good I kind of wanted to jump him right there in the middle of the department store. I'm sure that would have actually made his day. He didn't even blink an eye at the price of the suit, which for him was probably quite a lot of money.

"Thanks for doing this for me baby." I smiled, grabbing his free hand with mine.

"Naw, no problem. It was kind of fun, in a weird, awkward, there-was-definitely-a-gay-guy-checking-me-out-the-entire-time, kind of way." He smiled, leaning down to kiss me.

∞

That night I made good on my promise and let Aunt Dee try and help me cook. I think she almost jumped out of her moccasins when I asked if I could help her cook dinner.

"Why honey, I'd be honored!"

Blaine said he would be willing to miss his mom's cooking to try mine, but I could tell he was a little leery of it. He knew that my greatest masterpiece had been to make rice crispy treats, and even that I had messed up a couple times.

"Okay, what do I make?" I twirled my hair.

I was standing in the kitchen, my feet barefoot, and Aunt Dee standing in front of me. She was still a little sweaty from working at the shop all day and I hoped she planned to wash up before cooking.

"Well." Aunt Dee headed over to a cabinet and pulled out one of her cookbooks. "What's Blaine's favorite food?"

I thought for a moment, tapping my fingers on my chin. "Probably burgers and curly fries from Sam's."

Aunt Dee snorted. "Well I don't think that's something we can cook. How about gumbo?"

I shrugged. "Works for me."

So we spent the next hour laughing and cooking gumbo. I made a lot of mistakes and learned the proper way to chop vegetables. My mom and I never cooked together. I couldn't even remember making Christmas cookies or coloring Easter eggs as a child. Instead we went shopping. I never realized until that moment how much of a bonding affect it can have between people. Aunt Dee told me about the first time she cooked with her mom and even reminisced about cooking with Joni and Britt.

If someone would have told me a couple of months ago, that I would have cooked a meal for four people and they actually enjoyed it, I probably wouldn't have believed it. But I had. I had done something that people didn't question or laugh at me for.

When Blaine left that night he was still holding his stomach, saying how full he was after three helpings of my gumbo.

"Baby, I think there is hope for you being my southern belle after all." He leaned in meeting my gaze.

"I think I've still got some more to learn, but I'm willing to try." I wrapped my arms around him, sliding my body against his.

Lord help me, I was falling in love with the south. And even more, I was falling in love with a southern boy.

CHAPTER 20

After a week of playing over everything in my head, I realized that I was completely falling head over heels in love with Blaine. Which that wasn't the problem. The problem was actually telling him that.

It wasn't that I didn't have plenty of opportunities. We were still pretty much inseparable. It was just every time I would think it would be the perfect time to say it, I would choke up.

We would be laying together, him running his fingers through my hair, and a love song playing on the radio. I could say I love this song or I love root beer floats, but never the crucial I love you.

It wasn't like he ever said it either. He had just as much opportunity to say it as I did. Which is why I was kind of getting cold feet about saying it myself. He could give up smoking for me, and take the time off work to go back to my parent's with me, but he couldn't make the effort to say those three little words.

"Maybe he is scared for the same reasons you are."

Kristi seemed to be the only person I could talk to about this; she may have been scrambling with last minute wedding details. She may have been completely into herself, but she was the only person I knew I could talk to about it.

It wasn't like Britt had ever been in love or had a boyfriend, and I was sure that she wouldn't care to hear that I was in love with Blaine. And Aunt Dee, well that just wasn't something you talked about with your great-aunt.

There was my mom, but I didn't think that was a conversation to have with her either. She and my dad already didn't seem too thrilled I was bringing a boy home with me for Kristi's wedding. I didn't know if they were just so reluctant because of the last boy I brought home, Beau, or if they were just afraid I wasn't learning whatever lesson I was supposed to be learning in Louisiana.

And my real sister, Beth, well let's just say it would be less awkward talking to Aunt Dee than her.

So Kristi was my best choice. She was in love with Gabe and was getting married, so she had to have some good advice.

"What if he's not scared and actually secretly just hates me? And if I tell him I love him instead he'll just say that he hates me?" I pressed.

I was sitting alone in my room. It was that little stretch of time after dinner and before Blaine came, over when I could be alone. I had my door shut and was sitting on the floor, almost whispering so Aunt Dee and Britt couldn't hear me from the living room.

"Libby." She sighed. "I don't think any boy would quit smoking, and be willing to fly to Chicago for a wedding of someone he doesn't even know, if he hated you."

"Well how did you know the right time to say it to Gabe?" I pursued, lying down on the floor.

"Well." I could literally hear her thinking. There

were a lot of hmmms and ummms. "Gawd you know that was a long time ago, Libby. We've been together since freshman rush."

"That doesn't make me feel any better." I quipped, staring at my fingernails.

Kristi groaned. "Look Libby. If it is love, you'll just know the right time to say it. And even if it takes you years to say, if you know you love him, you don't have to broadcast the words to the world to let everyone know it. There are plenty of ways to show that you love someone without saying it."

"Do you think he's embarrassed to say it?" I sat back up, tilting my head.

Kristi laughed for a good minute. "Libby honey, just quit worrying about it! Let what happens, happen. And focus on other things. Like making sure you are all ready for my wedding in a couple of weeks."

I sighed. "Alright Kristi. Thanks for listening to me and yes, I am excited for the wedding. It's about time."

"LOL." Yes, she spoke in text. "Alright little, text me if you need anything else. I have another hair trial."

"Bye big."

Not too long ago I was worried because Blaine wouldn't sleep with me. That turned out fine. Better than fine actually. So I guessed being worried about him saying the L-word shouldn't be too hard either.

∞

One of my favorite things about nights in Louisiana was being able to stargaze. Sometimes I would feel like such a little girl. I loved to just lay in the grass and count the stars as lightning bugs would fly all around us. It may have been hot and mosquito ridden in Louisiana, but it still made me smile.

"Libby baby, you know for being a city girl you've seemed to adapt to the Bayou pretty well." Blaine smiled as he laid out the blanket

We found a place that was still on Blaine's property, but pretty far out. It was shaded by weeping willows, but there was a small hole in the tops of the trees that made it secluded and still gave us a good view of the stars.

I was digging my hand into a Tupperware container full of pralines. Blaine gave up on trying to make them, but his mom did a fabulous job. I knew that I was supposed to be trying to fit into my dress for the wedding, but I couldn't resist them.

"Hey, don't eat them all now baby!" He sprang up taking the container from me before plopping back on the blanket.

"I wasn't going to." I pouted, crossing my arms over my chest.

"I know." He patted the seat next to him. "I just wanted some for myself."

"Well you can't have them!" I laughed, jumping on top of him and knocking him down on onto his back on the blanket.

He almost dropped the pralines all over as I pinned his arms back behind his head.

"All of this for some pralines?" He smiled.

I leaned in so I was only about an inch from his face. "Yes, haven't you tasted them?" I could feel him exhale as I leaned and kissed him, still smiling.

He ran his fingers through my hair, looking into my eyes. "I don't think you realize how beautiful you are." His voice was like a southern lullaby.

"You southern boys." I whispered nuzzling his nose with mine.

"Do you have other boyfriends in Louisiana than just me?" He cocked an eyebrow.

Way to be Blaine and ruin my perfect moment to say it.

"Well." He rolled over so that he was now on top of me. "I guess if I have some competition."

Slowly he inched down, taking my shorts with him. He rolled back up and crept his fingers along my panty line, and then tugged them down with his mouth.

"Blaine." I propped up on my elbows. "You know I don't do outdoors. What if your mom walks out here?"

"No." He poked his head up from between my thighs. "You said no outdoor sex...this isn't technically sex..." Slowly he moved his fingers between my thighs.

It definitely wasn't something I could say no to. Especially when he was already down there. I also knew it could be my chance to finally just blurt out those words.

Just as I was at the point of climax, I moaned, "I...I...I love you."

I waited for what seemed like hours for him to say something. Hell, for him to even stop his tongue from what it was doing. But when I looked down, I couldn't see anything but his blonde mop of hair between my legs. Finally he put his head up and wiped his mouth, while rolling back over to the side of me. He laid on his back and propped his hands behind his head.

"And you said you didn't want any outdoors action." His eyes darted quickly in my direction before looking back up at the stars.

I just looked at him. It was like my eyes were just staring through him. Did he not hear me? I thought I was pretty loud. I kept pondering if I should say it again, or even ask him about it.

I shifted my body weight so that I was laying my head on his shoulder. He ran a free hand through my hair. I thought maybe he was waiting for his right moment too.

He opened his mouth then shut it again. We were silent for what seemed like forever, and then he reached his hand out and pointed upwards.

"Those stars kind of look like the big dipper."

"Yeah." I nodded, trying to blink the tears back.

CHAPTER 21

It had been a while since I had blurted out that I loved Blaine, and still he had said nothing about it. We were supposed to be leaving for Chicago together in about a week and I didn't know if I could do it. It had been like I was walking on eggshells all week.

Every time I would see him, it was hard for me not to scream, why don't you love me? It wasn't the easiest subject to just bring up to someone either. It wasn't like I could just walk up to him and say 'Hey Blaine, remember when you were going down on me and I said I love you?' Yeah that wasn't going to happen anytime soon.

The worst part about it, was that I felt like I had no one to talk to about it. Kristi was busy with her wedding, and besides Brittany, the only other real friend I had, in town, was Blaine.

I didn't want to look through search engines for answers or try and watch sappy love stories. Which trust me does not always work like you think it will. I just wanted the answer right there and now, so I turned to an unlikely source.

I was sitting at my desk, so I could still see Dina standing at the counter and checking her email. It wasn't like we talked too much on a normal basis. One would think since we had that talk weeks ago about Blaine that things would change. But we didn't really say much to each other unless she was asking about the budget, or telling me about some new thing she appraised.

This wasn't going to be easy. For a while I just sat there and stared at her. I couldn't believe that I was actually desperate enough to want to ask Dina for advice. But she seemed to know what she was talking about, and she must have loved Jackson (ignoring her infidelity of course).

With Beau, love was never a problem. I knew that I didn't love him and I think he knew he didn't love me as well. He would always say Love ya babe, but it was more of a term of endearment than anything. It meant nothing more than him saying 'Can you hand me another beer' or 'thank you.' I didn't want Blaine to think that's all it was when I said I loved him. It wasn't like a stupid crush or whatever Beau and I were. And now the problem was how to tell him…again…

"Hey Dina." I absently waved a hand as I stood in front of the counter

Dina recently decided to try contacts and would blink constantly, like a bird in flight, when she talked.

"Um." Blink, blink, blink. "Hi." Blink, blink, blink.

"Yeah." I bit down on my bottom lip shifting from one foot to the other. "I was just wondering if you had lunch plans."

"Don't you usually go off somewhere with Blaine for lunch?" She tapped a press-on nail clad fingertip against her teeth.

Maybe lunch wasn't such a good idea. I forgot how much she touches her lips and teeth. No, I had to be strong. This dilemma was killing me and I had to talk to someone about it.

"No, he actually has to work on the other side of the Parrish today, so he told me to just go get lunch without him."

Not a complete lie. He was working on the other side of the Parrish, but I actually texted him and said I was busy for lunch. He suspected nothing, oddly.

"So, yeah, how about pizza down the street at the bowling alley?" I shot a very weak smile.

She exhaled deeply. "Alright. I guess I've got nothing else to do for lunch."

She stood up. Her outfit was more hideous than usual. She had on a green khaki shirt dress, that showed way more cleavage that was appropriate for the office, and she was rather curvy. I wasn't even going to guess her bra size, but it was definitely a lot more than my barely B's. She also decided since it was summer, that it was still okay to pair some nude stockings with the dress, and hey stockings go great with open-toed gold sandals. She was pretty much a walking mess. But I was going to be nice. I knew that what I wore for band in high school wasn't exactly appealing, and if I was looking for advice, I couldn't be judgmental.

The bowling alley was a block away. It was nothing special. They had six lanes and it was upstairs from the post office. It was built in the 1950s and completely decorated in flamingo pink and mint green. The first time Blaine took me there I thought it was some sort of a joke, but it was definitely very real.

There was a small snack area that contained a pretty decent sized bar with a few pink tables and booths around it. For being a bowling alley it had pretty good pizza. And since Blaine worked there all through high school, he knew all the best places to sneak away to fool around. It may or may not have been a good thing that Dina and I were at the bowling alley for lunch.

"Is this where you always eat lunch?" Dina questioned as we started up the steps.

"No, but I find it to be a really cool place in a quirky sort of way." I was jabbering away nervously. "And besides, they have really good pizza and cheese fries."

She shrugged as we got to the top of the stairs. "If you say so."

Dina looked almost bored with me. She had already yawned and checked her cell phone about a dozen times since we left the office.

"Um, shall we order and then go grab a booth?" I pointed toward a corner booth near a really nostalgic-looking mint green juke box.

"Whatever." She shrugged again.

I was hoping the rest of our lunch would be a little bit more productive as I walked over to the counter.

I recognized the boy behind the counter, he couldn't have been more than sixteen and looked like one of the before pictures in a zit cream ad. I always caught him staring at me, and I think his voice squeaked even more when I came into the bowling alley.

"Hey Libby, is Blaine here?" He squeaked while looking behind me.

"No, just me and Dina today for lunch." I smiled, pointing my shoulders in the direction of Dina, who had simultaneously slid in beside me at the bar.

The boy behind the counter couldn't hide his smile as he grinned bigger than a Cheshire cat. "Oh, alright. Well, what can I get for you?"

Small towns: everyone seems to know who you are, where you live, and your pet's name.

"Um, well I am going to do the personal cheese pizza and a Diet Coke." I beamed. Maybe he'd give it to me free if I smiled enough at him.

"I'll have a catfish po'boy and a Mountain Dew." Dina said, still looking down, which didn't really matter because the boy didn't even take his eyes off of me.

"Alright I'll get that right up for you, Libby." His eyes didn't shift with that same goofy grin on his face.

"Okay." I nodded, trying to still force a smile and a small wave as Dina and I headed over to a booth.

"You know we haven't really, um, talked much lately." I tapped my fingers against the table. I was grasping at straws trying to think of what to say.

"It's true." She started blinking again furiously.

"Here are your drinks." The pimple-faced guy from the counter came over, almost tripping over his on feet while he slid the drinks onto our table. He still couldn't hide that grin. I was thinking that Blaine and I never got our drinks brought to us.

"Thanks Tripp." Dina sighed, still not looking up.

Tripp was still looking right at me. I flashed a weak smile. "Yeah, thanks."

"No problem, Libby. Your food will be right up!" He beamed and almost slipped again as he headed back to the bar.

"Well that was weird." I forced an awkward laugh.

"I'm sure you get that all the time." Dina mumbled before taking a big swig of her Mountain Dew.

"Not really." I took a sip of what I thought was Diet Coke, but was definitely Pepsi. It wasn't that I minded it, but someone should have told me.

"Actually, I don't."

She rolled her eyes. "Please Libby, ever since you came to town I think every boy has had a permanent hard-on."

Ouch, that was harsh. I thought Dina and I had some kind of kinship after our talk about Blaine and after she opened up to me about her past relationship. I guess I was wrong about that one.

"Well I don't think I'm going to be leaving Blaine for the bowling alley boy anytime soon. Of course he might leave me for the gutter ball girl, but that's up to him." I took a big gulp of my drink.

"What do you mean?" Dina finally looked up.

I couldn't hold it in anymore. It was like letting a huge weight off my shoulders. I spilled everything from being the ugly duckling in high school, Beau picking me out in a crowd at a fraternity party, my struggle with college, and meeting Blaine. By the time I wanted to get to my latest debacle with the 'L' word, Tripp had brought out our food.

I think Dina was happy for a break, the way her eyes actually didn't blink for about ten minutes straight, said it all. I was just happy that the bowling alley wasn't too busy and the whole town didn't hear my whole life story.

When Tripp left, after about a minute of gawking, I continued.

"I asked you to lunch because I didn't know who

else to turn to. I told Blaine that I loved him."

Dina almost choked on her sandwich. She quickly excused herself and wiped her mouth. "And? So now you're in love? Are you asking me if I can help him pick out a ring? I don't think you'd like my taste in jewelry."

"He actually didn't say it back." I took a quick bite of my pizza, muttering as I spoke.

"HE WHAT?"

Almost everybody, about all six people, at the bowling alley stared our way.

"Dina," I whispered.

Everyone quickly went back to what they were doing, pretending like they didn't hear us.

"Sorry Libby." She whispered, taking a quick drink. "But did I hear you right? You told him you loved him and he didn't say it back?"

I nodded.

"Well, what did he say?"

"Nothing." I took another bite of pizza and spoke with my mouth still half full, covering my mouth with my hand as I chewed that last bite.

"I mean, this is probably too much info, but it was during oral sex and I'm thinking maybe he just thought it was a reflex or something."

"Honey." She grabbed my hand. "No time a woman ever says 'I love you,' is it a reflex."

"I know." I took a deep breath. "But I don't know what I'm supposed to do. It's been out there for a while and he hasn't said anything!"

"Hmmm." Dina took another bite of her sandwich. "That is a tough one." She said it with a mouthful.

"I know! That's why I am sitting here with you, at

the bowling alley, and asking you what I should do."

"Well honey." She took a sip of her drink, clearing her throat. "I don't think I am the best one to be asking advice about love. You know my wrangling with it."

"I know Dina." I took another quick bite of pizza. "And that's one of the reasons I came to you. You had to have told Jackson you loved him at some point, and it had to have been reciprocated."

"That was a long time ago." She took a bite of her sandwich.

"Yeah, but I know you remember it. How did you tell him you loved him?" I leaned in closer.

"He actually said it first." A small smile crossed her lips.

"We started dating when I moved back into town. I was always a small town girl. I knew I would move back to Elsbury as soon as I graduated. Got a job at the antique shop and thought my life was set. Then out of the blue Jackson and I started talking. We were actually in a bowling league here that first summer I was back."

Dina nodded her head toward the lane before taking another sip of her drink.

"Anyway, after about the second night of bowling he asked me out on our first date and then we were inseparable. Like peanut butter and jelly," she mused.

"I do remember the first time I told him I loved him." Her eyes met mine, for what seemed like the first time all day.

"Really?" I almost choked on a mouthful of pizza.

"Yup." She nodded. "We were out on a Sunday morning, very early, fishing. It was about six a.m. and we had just rowed out. I was baiting my line when he just looked at me smiling. He then told me that he loves a girl that baits her own reel. I smiled, you know, thinking nothing of it. Then when I caught that first fish it was when he said that he loved me. Of course, I said it back right away, not knowing it would last another two and a half years and an almost engagement."

She looked down at that last part. That smile quickly escaped her face as she hastily stuffed it with her sandwich.

"I wish Blaine could have just said it first," I muttered taking a big bite of pizza.

"I'm sure it's not easy for him to say it, honey. He can act like the big, strong guy in his big truck all he wants, but you know Blaine. He's just a big softy and he does things when he wants." She nodded taking a bite of her sandwich.

"I mean, I guess you're right." I took a sip of my soda. "I mean, we didn't sleep together until he wanted to. Maybe he's just waiting for the right time to say it back. But don't you think he would have done something by now? It's been like a week."

Dina took a hard swallow of her sandwich. "Well then maybe you should just say it again and see what he does? You know get that whole romantic setting going and then see what he does. No orgasms scream, just say it, right to his face. You know, look him the eye." She pointed at me as she said eye.

I nodded. "You know you're right. That's what I gotta do." I smiled, leaning back in my seat. "You're so smart Dina."

"I know." She laughed and I joined her. It was the

first time I had actually laughed in a while, and I knew that I was going to do it. I was just going to get the balls and tell Blaine that I loved him…again…

CHAPTER 22

It was a Sunday, we were leaving for Chicago the next morning. Blaine's parents didn't mind that he missed church that morning when I came to help him pack, or distract him.

"Now baby, how am I supposed to concentrate on what to pack when you are lying on the bed like that?"

Blaine was on the floor in front of his bed, kneeling down at an old black suitcase. It was simple enough to pack as a guy: t-shirts, underwear, and socks. But somehow we convinced his parents it was important that I was there to help him finish packing. I was laying on his bed, flat on my stomach, my freshly-shaven legs dangling in the air.

I wouldn't say I was in the best shape, but the Louisiana sun had tanned my legs beautifully, making them a nice golden shade. Since I hadn't been, well, praying to the porcelain god, the color was definitely back in my cheeks.

"I'm just trying to direct you how to pack." I smiled, pointing a freshly manicured nail toward his suitcase.

"No." He leaned in placing a light kiss on my lips. "You are being a distraction."

"Is that a bad thing?" I pouted out my bottom lip.

"Well." He slowly stood up, making his way over to the bed. "I think you're the best damn distraction I ever had."

I pulled him down on top of me, and before we knew it, we were naked, entangled in each other. I was thinking this had to be some sort of a sin, sex while we should have been at church. But after the first orgasm, that was the farthest thing from my mind.

He finished quickly, but stayed there hovering over me. The sweat beaded on his forehead and he never took his eyes off of me. He rested on his elbows, leaning back.

I knew this was my chance. I looked into his eyes and ran my fingers through his hair.

"I love you."

There was no way he could deny it, or pretend like he didn't hear me. He was looking right back at me. Hell, he was still in me.

And yet he said nothing. He just pulled out of me and stood up, turning his back to me while he pulled off the condom, tossing it into the trash near his bed.

"Um?" I sat up, and patted him on the shoulder. "Do orgasms make you deaf? Or did you just not hear me?"

"No, I heard you." His back was still to me while he grabbed his boxers and shorts, sliding them on.

"And yet, you have nothing to say?" I was still completely naked, rising from the bed and putting my hands to my hips.

"Baby..." He exhaled deeply and put his shirt on, finally turning toward me.

"Baby what?" I stomped to the end of the bed,

snatching my panties and shorts. "I've told you that I love you twice, and you have just said nothing!"

My fingers fumbled as I tried to put my bottoms on. I was starting to get angry and my mind was not working with my fingers.

He sighed and slowly stepped toward me. "Libby..."

I stepped back when I finally got my shorts buttoned. It was hard to argue standing there shirtless, so I crossed my arms over my chest.

"Libby what? Let me hear what you got to say for yourself!"

He sighed again, covering his face with his hands. He was became a pro at the sighing thing. "That's not just a word I want to throw around, Libby."

"So if you tell me you love me it's just throwing a word around? You don't mean it?" I put my hands back on my hips, taking a step toward him.

The truth was that I loved Blaine, no matter how much he made me mad. Even at that exact moment, I was still crazy about him. I loved the way he stared me down with those big blue eyes, every time I saw him, especially all of his sun tanned body, I couldn't help but smile. It hurt more than anything that this person, that I had so many feelings for, couldn't say anything back.

He put his hands up and out in front of him. "Whoa, that's not what I am saying, Libby."

"Then what are you saying, Blaine?" I was trying to fight back tears and I slid on my tank top.

"Libby." He tried to grab my hand, but I pulled away. "You know I care about you, hell I wouldn't be going to Chicago with you if I didn't. I wouldn't have given up smoking, or took every lunch hour I had, to be with you."

I stopped fiddling with my shirt and looked straight at him. For once his steel blue eyes didn't scare me or entice me, and I just looked right through them.

"But do you love me, Blaine?"

He looked away and sat down on the bed, putting his face in his hands. "I don't know." He glanced up at me, his eyes intensely blue.

"I care about you a whole lot, Libby. You are an amazing girl. You make me happier than I have been in a long time."

"But." I took another step forward so that I was right in front of him. I looked down, hands folded across my chest. "Do you love me?" I over-enunciated every word.

He didn't answer. He didn't even look at me. I wiped my eyes with the back of my hand as the tears started to form. "Well, I guess I have my answer."

He didn't say anything, he didn't even follow me as I walked down the stairs. I didn't look back as I ran from his house all the way back to Aunt Dee's. By the time I got there I was soaking wet, partly from sweat and partly from sobbing almost the whole way home. I had to stop so much, since my tears were blurring my vision.

By the time I got home it had been almost half an hour since I had left Blaine's. My purse was sitting on the porch. A small note scribbled out on a piece of notebook paper sat on top of it with a simple note reading, call me.

I crumbled up the piece of paper and threw it away

once I got inside. I didn't call him and he didn't call me that night. I went to bed still in tears.

CHAPTER 23

The flight for Chicago left New Orleans at eight a.m. Since it was always a mess to get through the airport, we had to leave the house at four just to make sure we got there in time.

Blaine was supposed to be at the house by three, and with him always being early I expected him there at quarter till. By the time three o'clock rolled around, he still wasn't there. I didn't call him the night before and he didn't call me.

Three fifteen hit and Aunt Dee was getting nervous. But I still sat there on the porch swing, waiting for his truck to pull in the driveway, and for everything to be all better. I thought it would be like that night after the Fourth of July. He would just show up at my door, kiss me, and make everything all right. But this time it didn't happen.

At four fifteen Aunt Dee told me we couldn't wait anymore. She assured me that maybe he was planning on meeting us at the airport, and he overslept or something. She said I should try calling him again, but I still couldn't bear to do it. I didn't even want to hear his voice on his voicemail, so I sent one single text.

Leaving. I love you and hope that you show up at the

airport.

∞

We rode almost in silence to the airport. It was just Aunt Dee and I. She didn't ask any more questions about Blaine, and I was so grateful for that. After my bags were checked and she had to leave me at the terminal, we both looked around one last time. We both knew what we were looking for. It was six-thirty. We would be boarding in about an hour and Blaine still hadn't arrived, or returned my text.

"Well Libby...I have to get going...I have to get to the shop..."

Her green eyes were looking all around instead of right at me. I knew what she was thinking, what she was praying. She hoped that Blaine would show up. I half-wondered if she was hoping he would show up more than I did. But she didn't ask anything more about him. She didn't even bring him up. She just finally looked right at me and smiled a tight lipped smile.

"I know Aunt Dee. I will call you when I get home and promise to be back next Sunday."

I reached down and hugged her. At full height she came just below my chest, so I had to lean in a lot to make it an actual worthwhile hug. I almost felt comfort in her smell now. The smell of Spanish moss and sweat didn't bother me as much as it did that first night. It lingered like a memory. I never thought I would fall in love in Louisiana, with a person or with the area itself, and it was like leaving home all over again to go back to Chicago.

At seven-thirty they called for final boarding. I looked around the airport again, hoping maybe Blaine would come running. He would put his arms around me and envelope me in his arms. Telling me that he had overslept and he was so sorry, and then finally say those three little words.

But none of that happened.

I took a deep breath and made one last call, before boarding the plane, it went straight to voicemail.

Hey it's Blaine, obviously I can't come to the phone right now, so do what you gotta do at the beep.

His voice seemed so far away. It was like I was underwater and he was just standing over me, trying to get my attention. But I couldn't raise my head above it and was just treading below.

I didn't know what to say in the voicemail. Hell, I didn't even know what I would have said if he would have picked up. So I wiped my eyes and put on a fake smile, leaving the only message I could think of.

"Hey It's Libby. Um, boarding the plane now. Hope to see you in Chicago. Um, yeah, bye."

I turned off my phone and boarded the plane, situating in my seat for the ride back to Chicago. Back to a life where I didn't know who I was: Big Bird, sorority princess, or just Libby. In a few short hours I would find out.

∞

My sister, Beth, and I were kind of like Arnold Schwarzenegger and Danny Devito in the movie

Twins. She was flawless. She had long blonde hair that was wavy and not frizzy, like mine. Her height didn't gawk people, she was petite, with a face and chest that most women spent thousands of dollars at the plastic surgeon to get.

When I saw her at the terminal gate she looked more radiant than ever. I think she was one of the few people who I could say that married life had been good to. Last year she had married her longtime boyfriend, Ben, who was almost 10 years her senior and an established chiropractor in the city. Needless to say, he spoiled her rotten. Working as a kindergarten teacher was almost a hobby, since she really didn't need to work. Even at five years older than me, people still always thought she was my younger sister.

As soon as saw me she squealed with delight and enveloped me in her tiny arms. I think her ginormous breasts crushed my belly button.

"My, my, Libby, look at you! I think the south has done you some good!" She put her tiny fists on the waist of her designer jeans and gave me the once over.

Compared to her I probably looked like a bag lady standing there. I was exhausted partly from crying all night, and partly since I had to be up so early. I was clad in nothing more than cropped sweat pants and a tank top. The belly that I had developed over the summer felt like it was protruding over my pants.

Then of course I had to stand next to the perfectly put together Barbie herself. She sure got dressed up just to pick someone up at the airport: jeans that probably cost more than I made in a week, heels, and a black cowl neck t-shirt. I was actually pretty sure this was her weekend wear.

"So where is this Louisiana boy you've been raving about?" She looked past me. "Is he back there carrying your luggage for you like a good southern gentleman?"

"Um..." I bit down on my lower lip, looking down at my sister.

The truth was I turned on my phone as soon as they pilot announced it was safe to do so, hoping for a message from Blaine saying 'I missed my flight', or 'overslept.' I didn't get either of that. I did get a text from him though, two words.

I'm sorry.

That was it. Not a phone call, not an excuse, just those two words. Not the two words that I was really looking for.

"Libby, this isn't like that Brady Bunch episode where Jan made up a boyfriend is it?" Beth cocked an eyebrow at me.

I couldn't help but smile at that one.

"No." I sighed and the smile erased from my face. "It's a bit more complicated than that."

"Well." She threw an arm around me, which was literally a throw since the top of her head barely reached my shoulders.

"We can talk about that on the hour ride it's going to take us to get out of the airport."

I shook my head and forced a weak laugh. Too bad the situation actually wasn't funny.

∞

"So he just didn't show up?" Beth shrieked while she tried to back her Mercedes out of the parking spot.

I explained, mostly everything, by mostly I mean, not much at all. I told her we had a fight, but I didn't exactly say what the fight was about and neglected to mention anything about the unreciprocated love.

"Nope, he just left me waiting." I fiddled with the buckle on my seatbelt.

We were definitely back in the city, this wasn't like small town New Orleans, and I never thought I would miss it so much. I was surrounded by sky scrapers and angry drivers, instead of the willow trees and slow talking locals.

But most of all I missed Blaine. I wanted him to be there sitting in the backseat of my sister's car. I wanted to look back and see him smile while I pointed and told him what every single building was that we passed. But instead I sat there in silence. Of course, the car wasn't completely silent. My sister not only liked to blare her music, but she also never knew a conversation she didn't like. Even if it was one that was basically with herself.

On a good day my parents' house was about thirty minutes from the city and forty-five minutes from the airport. Our neighborhood didn't have the small European style houses of Louisiana. It was the same cookie cutter, suburban homes, and row after row of them.

After I graduated high school, my parents tried to sell our five bedroom house to move into a condo in the city, but with the economy the way it was, nothing was selling. So it was just the two of them, and of course their French Bulldog, in the big house. Our neighborhood was the same as many of the North Shore community homes. We enjoyed views of Lake Michigan and neighbors with homes in the millions. The homes were modeled after beach houses, since we were walking distance from the beach.

"Are you sure you don't want to go to lunch? Or even just to come to the house to hang out?" Beth stared at me.

We had pulled into the cobblestone driveway about five minutes ago, but she had sat there trying to convince me to hang out with her. I really couldn't hide things from my sister very well. Even though we were five years apart, we were still very close. She was always a friend to me growing up. Even though she was always the popular blonde, she always made time for her outcast little sister.

"Yeah, I'm really tired Beth. You know I had to get up early to make it to the airport and all." It was partly true, I was tired, but more about the fact that I couldn't sleep the night before. I was also hoping that Blaine would call, text, or something. And if he did I didn't want my sister to be around.

"Alright, well Ben and I will be over in a couple of hours for dinner. Mom's ordering Mongolian!" She yelled out the car window as I got out.

Mom didn't cook. Googling a new restaurant was her idea of trying a new recipe.

I ran up to the front door and my sister didn't drive away until I was able to get in. I waved as I securely unlocked the door and pushed it open, thrusting my suitcase in ahead of me.

The cleaning lady had definitely already been there. The large crystal chandelier that hung above the foyer sparkled onto the hardwood floor and out the large windows. I think you could have fit Aunt Dee's whole house into our foyer and dining room. It was only two o'clock in the afternoon, my parents wouldn't be home until at least six.

I kind of wished I did have some company. The house couldn't have felt emptier. I shut the door and left my suitcase in the foyer as I headed toward the kitchen. It looked like my mom had remodeled again. This time I guessed that granite was the new black. Granite countertops and stainless steel flooded the kitchen. I felt like I was inside of an industrial warehouse, and with the size of my parents' kitchen it probably could have been one.

My stomach was rumbling. I opened the fridge, but just as I expected nothing but some condiments and leftover Chinese food. I grabbed a container and smelled its contents. It didn't seem like it was too old and I was sure that the cleaning lady would have thrown it out if it was. I popped the container, which looked like it had some sort of lo-mein in it, into the microwave and looked at my phone again.

Blaine hadn't called, texted, Facebooked, e-mailed, nothing. I thought about calling my mom and letting her know I was in, but it was Appeals Monday and I knew she would be busy.

I could hear rumblings from the laundry room. I knew my mom usually didn't let the dog out during the day, but I figured this was a special occasion. I went into the laundry room to see my little French Bulldog up on her hind legs in the cage. Her tongue was hanging out of her mouth as she whimpered.

Sally, the dog, was a thirteenth birthday gift from my parents. I had begged for a dog for years, but they always said it was too messy, but finally they gave in. When I first saw Sally, I thought she was the ugliest thing I had ever seen. But she grew on me, and grew even more on my dad. Once I left for college she kind of took over as my dad's dog and usually never left his side at night.

That didn't mean she wasn't happy to see me. Once I let her out of the cage, she licked my face and pranced her way after me into the kitchen.

The timer went off on the microwave and I carried the container and a fork upstairs to what was my bedroom. Sally happily following behind me. My mom, or should I say the cleaning lady, had left it exactly as I left it. My sleigh bed was in the center as a focal point with a deep maroon comforter overtaking it. It wasn't the twin bed with the bubblegum bedspread that I had become accustomed to. I took a bite of my lo-mein as I headed toward my balcony.

We were lucky enough that each of our bedrooms had French doors that led to a small balcony. Of course there wasn't much room for anything else but two people to stand on the balcony. But I enjoyed getting somewhat of a sun tan out there for the past nineteen summers. I looked out and could see that the gardeners were out making sure every blade of grass was mowed and every flowerbed was weeded. It really wasn't fair that they were out there in the heat. I guess that was their job, and I felt like I was kind of abandoning mine. But I was here for a reason, not just because I got in a fight with Blaine, but for Kristi's wedding.

I walked back into my bedroom and set the lo-mein on the dresser, ironically next to the picture of my parents and me at my first day of school. I took my phone out of my pocket. I sent a quick I'm here text to Kristi and set my phone down.

I knew she would probably want to go out later, and I knew my parents would want to spend time with me. It really was great that so many people were glad that I was home, but all I could really think about was how much I wished Blaine was with me. So I fell asleep to dream of his blue eyes.

∞

I woke up to the sound of my mom's heels clicking on the hardwood floor in the hallway. I knew it would be a while before she got to my bedroom, but I decided I should at least try and get up.

Sally was already up before I could even lift my head off the pillow. She happily pounced off of the bed and her little paws padded on the wood floor while she waltzed over to my bedroom door.

My mom picked Sally up as she walked into the room. After not seeing my mom for a few months she looked different to me. She seemed to have a whole new glow about her, or maybe that was Botox. My mom, my sister, and I all had the same strawberry blonde hair. Except my mom, I noticed, had wisps of gray around her temples, the same shade of gray as Sally's fur.

I wondered if she noticed them, or if for some reason they matched her Dolce & Gabbana glasses to make her look distinguished. I honestly wasn't even sure that my mom needed glasses, but I think she thought people would take a blonde lawyer more seriously if she had glasses.

"Hey Libby. Beth called and told me about the boy." She sat down on the end of my bed putting Sally down beside her. "Dad said he's willing to go down to Louisiana and pull him here by his bicuspids if you would like."

I smiled a genuine smile at my mom. "No, that's fine, I think I can handle this one on my own."

She reciprocated that smile, showing her teeth that could only be the dream of any dentist. I honestly think that's why my dad married her. She had perfect teeth and he wanted to pass that gene down.

"Come on, let's go downstairs and see what we can decipher that might be good to order from this Mongolian restaurant."

She motioned her hands for me to get up. Life may be confusing, but always leave it to a mother to fix things with humor and food.

∞

Dad got home just as Mom, Beth, and I were getting the table set. Mom and I had to Google a lot of the food on the menu to see what it actually was and after that Mongolian food didn't seem as enticing as we thought it would be. But we settled on some buuz, which are meatballs twisted Hershey Kiss style into ravioli type pasta and steamed boodog, which was goat cooked with hot stones in it. Then we got added rice and a few butter cookies. I thought southern food was weird at first, but this definitely wasn't anything like gumbo.

"Well I see your mom tried a new restaurant." Dad smiled while he kissed Beth and me on the cheek.

Dad seemed to have a new radiance to him as well. I was wondering if they both went and got a two for one deal on Botox. My sister whispered that it was because they were having more sex since I was gone. I shuttered at that thought.

"So Libby, has Elsbury made a southern belle out of you yet?" My dad asked as he spooned some goat onto his plate.

I winced. Blaine always called me a southern belle. "Um, well I helped Aunt Dee make a praline pie once, so I think I'm on my way!"

"There are actually women in this family that cook?" Ben, my sister's husband, joked between mouthfuls of food.

Ben was quite a bit older than my sister, and his age really showed. Physically he was really fit. He worked out I think, more than anyone, and in fact he actually met my sister by taking her spinning class at the gym one summer. But even with his vast knowledge of all things NCAA he still couldn't hide that he just wasn't up on the times. This included his wardrobe. That man owned more pairs of white Reeboks and sweatpants, than anyone over thirty ever should.

"Aunt Dee is a really amazing cook." I beamed. "Probably the best in the whole Parrish."

"Yeah, it looks like you haven't missed too many of

her meals either." My dad smiled.

My mom and sister froze. I don't think either of them were completely oblivious to the events of the past year. I remembered last Thanksgiving where my mom witnessed me eating an entire pumpkin pie, and then spend the next half an hour in the guest bathroom with the water on. But for some reason it actually didn't faze me. I just smiled back at my dad and took another huge bite of lamb. I wasn't scared of what fights could ensue or anything else my parents could throw at me.

"Well, we do actually have a reason that we gathered you all here tonight." My mom grabbed my dad's hand.

"Oh, us first!" Beth protested, pounding her fist on the table like a little kid.

"Alright Beth, I guess you first." My dad smiled, taking a big gulp of his water. I noticed he didn't have a glass of bourbon or scotch or any alcohol, odd. I was surprised that he didn't get angry either.

"Well." Beth beamed at Ben and grabbed his hand. "Ben and I are expecting a little bundle of joy!"

She looked back at us.

My dad almost choked on his water and my mom squealed with delight. Before I knew it, everyone was jumping around the table and hugs and kisses were flying about. I honestly had no idea that they were even trying, or hell, that he could still shoot straight. I found out her due date was in March, so she was about a month and a half pregnant. She had been keeping it in for that past couple of weeks so she could wait until everyone was together to tell us.

It was actually kind of nice that she wanted to

include me. I didn't know if it was a good thing or a bad thing that Blaine wasn't there. He was an uncle himself, but this was something that was my own. My first time being an aunt, and I knew that baby would be more spoiled than any other living creature.

The screaming and hugging went on for what seemed like hours before we all sat back down and mom cleared her throat to get all of our attention.

"Okay, now for our news!" My mom clasped her hands together as she sat back down at the table.

"Your father and I have finally sold the house. We close at the end of the month and finally get to move into the condo at Trump tower!" she spilled with delight.

"Well, will there be enough room for the baby when we visit?" Beth questioned. I loved my sister, but of course Beth was always first.

"There are three bedrooms, and a den. So we should have enough room for Libby, the baby, and an office." My dad smiled.

"Um, well you probably don't have to worry too much about a room for me. I can just get an air mattress when I come home," I said between bites of lamb.

"Well you'll need a bedroom, Libby where else are you supposed to stay while you go to school?" My mom cocked an eyebrow.

I wasn't sure what to say. My goal of the summer was ultimately to get back into school, but now I didn't know what I wanted. To go back to Louisiana and work at the antique shop forever? Maybe try and get back into Illinois State? I was still treading water and coming back home made me feel like I was drowning.

"Well, that's something we can discuss later." My dad changed the subject. Obviously I wasn't a high priority. "Tonight we celebrate!"

He raised his glass and we all clinked ours together. My sister was having a baby, my parents were getting a new house, and I was rejected by my boyfriend. What a day to celebrate.

CHAPTER 24

Kristi wanted to take all of her bridesmaids out a couple days before the wedding to The Pleasant Hill Spa to have a day of pampering. And of course to get beautified for her wedding. I started putting on sweat pants and a tank top, since it was a spa I thought I should be comfortable, and then realized I was in Chicago and going out with a bunch of sorority girls. It was like that first night in Louisiana. I thought my image was everything and I knew they would be judging me by it. I instead put on a pair of jeans and a white tank top. I didn't have time to do anything with my hair and figured that shouldn't matter too much. I just threw it up in a ponytail as I headed out the door.

The spa was out on the North Shore, so it wasn't too far from my parents' place. It had been awhile since I drove through town and was like going through a different world. I longed for the willow trees and swamp grass of Elsbury, and even more I really wanted Blaine at my side.

But I put on a happy face as I ran through the doors of the spa. This was going to be the same resort that Kristi would be getting married at in just a few days; as she would tell us over and over. I couldn't miss the girls when I walked in. Leave it to a bunch of sorority girls to be completely made up to go to the spa.

"Libby LOL, we were hoping you didn't get stuck in the swamp or something!" Kristi screamed and ran over to me. I wish she would just say laugh out loud instead of abbreviating it or even just laugh or something, but that was Kristi.

Kristi was also the type of girl that didn't leave the house unless she was completely made up. Her red hair was newly highlighted with blonde streaks and perfectly straightened before put in a bumped up ponytail that had to take her hours. But she made it look messy as if she only took a few minutes to do it. Since she was a natural redhead she didn't tan and the orange glow about her was obviously from a spray tan. And even though we were supposed to be getting facials and massages, she couldn't help but layer on the liquid eyeliner and foundation. I guess one needs liquid eyeliner to match a hot pink bride t-shirt?

"Hey Kristi." I smiled, doing a weak little wave.

"Oh my, look at what the south has done to your hair!" She took her tiny hands to tousle my ponytail. "Someone forgot to pack her straightener!"

The rest of the bridal party giggled in the background.

"Well I guess that's why I'm at the spa." I shrugged.

"Now, is that hunk of southern man with you or did you leave him at home with the dog?" She stood on her tippy toes to look around me.

"I saw his pictures on Facebook. Sign me up for one of those!" One of the other bridesmaids piped up.

"Um..." I bit on my lower lip looking down. "He actually didn't come to Chicago at all," I whispered.

"Oh."

Everyone got really quiet for a minute before the lady at the front desk called our party back for manicures. I was glad for the interruption, but knew that wasn't the end of it.

∞

We were getting our pedicures. Kristi sat two girls down from me and I had another sorority sister on each side. Kristi was the golden only child, so her wedding was not only an elaborate jester, but everything down to the bridal party was big. There were ten of us and we took up the entire room.

"So, I guess Beau's been asking about you all summer." Lacey, who was next to me in the chair, poked me with a freshly manicured nail.

"Yeah, and?" I leaned back in my chair as the lady scrubbed my foot furiously with pumice.

"Well he is going to be at the wedding tomorrow and you know, since it doesn't look like you have a date," she remarked.

Not only was Beau not someone I wanted to talk about, but Lacey was one of his many little trysts. Of course she says it was all a big mistake. They were really drunk at a party. But when you think about sisterhood, I don't really think you should be sleeping with your sister's boyfriend. Of course, being the timid Libby, I was trying to please everyone. I just shrugged it off and accepted her apology. Now I realize I shouldn't have been such a pushover.

"I think I would rather go dateless, than ever touch Beau again with anything less than a ten foot pole covered in saran wrap."

The girls all ooh'ed followed by a round of giggles.

"It looks like the south gave Libby some balls." Another girl quipped, again followed by a round of giggles.

"But really Libby," Kristi piped in. "What happened with Louisiana boy anyway? I mean, from your Facebook statuses I thought things were going good."

I would have discussed this with Kristi, but the truth was I really didn't want to. She gave me the advice to tell him that I loved him, that didn't work. In all reality I felt like she didn't really care what happened with Blaine and me. I wasn't saying she was a selfish person, but the only child syndrome really turned her into a bridezilla. Twice today I had seen her scream at an employee, and not just raise her voice, but an all-out nostril flare screaming.

"You know, I guess it was just a summer fling or whatever." I shrugged, hoping soon the subject would go back to Kristi.

"Speaking of summer love." Lacey piped.

Kristi's phone started ringing. Of course her ring tone was the bridal march. Gag.

"It's Gabe!" She squealed before putting the phone to her ear.

"Hey Gabey, I missed you so much!" She cooed in a baby voice.

I almost kicked the lady at my feet. That was almost exactly what I said to Blaine in the bar when I was trying to make a show in front of his ex.

Kristi went on with her baby talk before she said her good byes and went on for about five minutes of 'No you hang up first.' I was stunned. Kristi had a degree in business finance, not just some blow off degree, but a genuine business degree. She was on the honor roll and even did an internship with a Fortune 500 company. But for her fiancé or her sorority sisters, she turned into a thirteen-year-old girl.

And then it hit me. That's what I had turned myself into the past school year, and that wasn't me. The realest I had ever felt was when I was in Louisiana. When Aunt Dee let me do the books, no one else had ever had the confidence in me. And when Blaine would talk to me, he wasn't trying to dumb anything down, or trying to just use flirtatious jokes to get what he wanted. No, he wanted to talk to me, Libby. The real Libby Gentry.

∞

After dinner with the girls it was getting pretty late. They wanted to go downtown, but I told the girls my parents wanted me home early. I lied, but I had to make a phone call and it was the only call where I was for sure, I would get some answers.

"Hey, you were the last person I was expecting to get a call from."

I could hear the low voices of the evening news in the background while Dina spoke. I knew she would be home on a Wednesday night.

"Yeah, I know, but friends call each other right?"

I was sitting alone in the McDonalds parking lot. Almost everywhere had laws against driving and talking on cell phones, and I didn't want to go home to have this conversation. I thought I'd better be safe than sorry.

"What do you want, Libby? No, Blaine hasn't come over and tried to seduce me." Her voice sounded annoyed.

"Have you seen him or heard anything about him?" I figured she had to have heard some sort of gossip. It was a small town after all.

"All of us sure were surprised when you left for Chicago without him." I could hear her almost whistling through her snaggleteeth.

"I've tried everything Dina!" I was almost in tears now.

"I've called, texted, e-mailed, Facebook messaged. And still I've heard nothing. And I want to come back to Elsbury more than anything. I love working at the shop. I love living with Aunt Dee, and I truly love Blaine. I just..." A single mascara-ridden tear fell down my facial. "I don't know what to do."

I could hear her breathing deeply. It was almost a full minute before she finally answered. "I'm only doing this because I like you." She rambled off a number.

"Dina, I don't need some sort of booty call," I protested, wiping my face with the back of my hand.

"It aint no booty call, that's Jackson's number. Blaine should be over there or at least with Jackson. If he's not, Jackson should have some answers."

"Do you think he'll pick up for me?" I sniffled.

"Well there is only one way to find out."

∞

I couldn't call right away. I just didn't have it in me

and it was hard to get up the courage to do it. So I drove home. Before entering the house I made sure I didn't look like a hot mess. I, of course, after spending a day at the spa, did look like an overdone beauty queen. But that was about the end of it.

It was nine o'clock. Mom was upstairs in her office going over some files and Dad was sitting in front of the TV watching a Cubs game, but strangely not a single drop of liquor to be found.

I tried to slowly creep past him, not to disturb him. I didn't want to be lectured or have to answer a million questions.

"Hey, Libby."

I stopped and did an about face toward the den, popping my head in, hoping to quickly get up to my bedroom.

"Hey, Dad."

He patted the seat next to him on the couch, something he hasn't done since I was in middle school. I reluctantly crossed the room and sat down next to him.

I didn't want a lecture and that's what I was afraid was coming, but instead he smiled.

"You know Libby, I have been keeping in contact with Aunt Dee whether you know it or not, and I just want you to know that I am really proud of you."

I almost choked on my own saliva. I didn't remember my dad ever saying he was proud of me. Hell, or even seeing my dad sitting around without a glass of some sort of brown liquid in his hand.

"You know in high school you were insecure. You just poured yourself into your music and then just labeled yourself as a band geek. Then you go off to college. I think, you know things will change she'll find herself there." He shrugged.

He then turned toward me. In truth there were a lot of features that I had of my mom's, but no one could deny that my dad and I had the same brown eyes. His eyes were usually full of fury, but this time they had softened as he looked at me. I guess I not only had my dad's height, but I had his smile as well.

"Then you go to Louisiana, which I expect to be a punishment, and you'd be begging to come back and start working at my office. But you didn't. You stuck it out and it's really made you the young woman that I always thought you were."

He patted my knee and looked off dreamily.

"My mom loved Elsbury, you know. And she was a lot like you when she was younger. Then she fell in love with a boy from the North and moved us up here and they said she left her wild past. The love of her life really changed her, made her the woman she always knew she was."

He looked down at me.

"Now I'm not saying go off and marry this Blaine kid, or that you should run off with him. But what I am saying is that I am happy with what Elsbury has made of you, and I think it's the woman I always knew you were. You left Chicago a girl and you became a woman."

He stopped talking and patted my knee.

"Now come here and give your old man a kiss so we can stop this sappy moment." He smiled and opened his arms.

They were some of the nicest words my dad had ever said to me, and I knew I had to make that phone call to Jackson.

Slowly I crept back up to my room and closed the door. Sally of course, was right at my heels and happily licked my wrists once she jumped on the bed next to me.

I had the number written on a crumbled napkin and I slowly punched in the number. It was now or never.

"Y'ello, this is Jackson." A slow, southern drawn voice called.

"Hey Jackson, its Libby."

I could hear voices in the background and the sound of the TV. Some sort of video game was being played. I could hear Blaine's voice over everyone else's. Maybe it was just because it was the one I was used to the most.

"Hey, hold on just one sec." I could hear him moving as he spoke. Soon the voices inside the house had stopped and I heard the creak of a door, and the chirps of grasshoppers and other nightly creatures.

"Libby if you really needed a date to the wedding that bad you should have asked me before Blaine. I already own a suit," He joked.

I couldn't help but smile. "No Jackson, that's not why I called."

"I know, I know. You like them blonde and moody," he quipped. "Well if you want to know the truth, the boy is miserable. Anytime he sees any sort of tall blonde girl I'm afraid he's going to start yelling your name."

"Really?" I sat up and Sally stirred in my lap.

"Libby you know the boy's in love with you. I've tried to talk to his stupid ass about it, but he just keeps ignoring it, changing the subject or grunting."

"Well, what am I supposed to do? He's the one that stood me up at the airport. I put my heart out there." I tried to maintain my composure, and I really had to stop this being on the brink of tears thing.

"Libby, darling. The boy may look like a tough ol' guy, but he's honestly just a big puppy that didn't want to be left alone in the backyard again. So he thinks if he runs now he won't get left alone."

Leave it to Jackson to use dog analogies.

"Hold on one second honey." I could hear him set the phone down. It had to be on something rusted because it creaked through the speaker.

Then more creaking in the background and muffled voices before someone picked the phone back up.

"Hello?"

It was Blaine. My heart stopped. I couldn't breathe.

"Uh, hello? Is anyone there?"

"Blaine? It's me." I whispered.

I was afraid he would hang up, or just say something horrible. He didn't. Instead the sound of crickets grew louder and the sound of his work boots against the pavement rattled over the phone.

"Libby?" He questioned.

"Look Blaine. I hate what you did to me. I hate the fact that you couldn't say that you loved me back. I hate it even more that you felt like since we had an argument you couldn't still come with me to Kristi's wedding. But the truth is, whether you love me or not, I still want you here. I still want you in my life."

"Libby, I don't know what to say. All I can really say is that I'm sorry. I fucked up big this time." His voice almost squeaked with nervousness.

"I can forgive you Blaine. I really want to. You're my biggest reason for wanting to come back to Elsbury. I miss the south. I miss Aunt Dee, but most of all I miss you," I blurted.

"Can you honestly say that you love me, Libby? After all the hell I've put you through?" I could hear him pacing. His boots crunched against the pavement of Jackson's back patio.

"From our first meeting when I called you names, to our fights about sex, to me not telling you that I loved you; can you say that after all that, you still love me?" I could hear him breathing, it was heavy and slow. It was a lot of emotion for him at once. I didn't think any guy is really good with any kind of emotion, and every time we did fight, he usually handled it with frustration. This was the first time I actually heard him just lay it all out on the line.

"Blaine." I started slowly getting off of my bed and headed out toward the balcony.

I looked up at the stars. It was the same stars I had looked at the first time I told Blaine that I loved him, and my feelings still hadn't changed.

"I may be angry. I may be hurt. But, undeniably I am still in love."

CHAPTER 25

It was the night of Kristi's rehearsal. I hadn't heard from Blaine since our phone call two nights before. But I was trying to put that behind me. Truth is, even though Blaine wasn't calling, Beau was blowing up my phone with texts and phone calls.

He was the last person I wanted to see, but I knew that he was one of Gabe's groomsmen and I was pretty sure that we were going to be walking together in the wedding.

I wished I could have just worn jeans and a t-shirt to show Beau that I wasn't there to impress him. But I wouldn't do that to Kristi. I also wasn't fitting very well into my jeans, so I settled for a bohemian style maxi dress and let my hair just fall into its natural wave. I knew the other bridesmaids would be going all out in their designer dresses, but at this point I really didn't care what they thought.

The rehearsal was back at the resort, so I drove my little sports car there. It was like a whole new world filled with Bentleys and Jaguars. I would have given anything just to turn my car around and head south, toward Louisiana. Just go right back to how things were, spending my days at work and nights with Blaine.

But I was a big girl. It was time to put on my big

girl panties and face the likes of spoiled rich girls, and worst of all my ex-boyfriend.

Luckily this time I wasn't late, but there weren't too many people there yet. The wedding was taking place on the beach. I could feel the lake breeze greet me as I walked to the back of the resort. Kristi was in full bridezilla mode at that point. Her nostrils were flared and she was pointing at some poor staff member. I made my way toward where the other bridesmaids were standing and whispered to Lacey.

"What's going on?"

She smiled and leaned in toward me, not taking her eyes off of Kristi.

"Someone got the wrong shade of white for the aisle runner." Her breath already smelled of vodka. It looked like the party had started early.

I was shocked when Kristi decided to get married on the beach. She was the most put together person I had ever met and I could not imagine her with sand between her toes. But I guess that's why the aisle runner was so important. No sand for the toes.

Lacey looked back at me, her green eyes scanning me. She was very petite, probably about five foot three, so it took her a while to scan all of me. She took a sip of her drink and then twirled a strand of her auburn hair, smirking.

"Cute dress, who is it by?"

"Um." I bit my bottom lip, scratching at the back of my neck. "I don't know, whatever Wal-Mart brand is?"

She almost dropped her glass while the rest of the bridal party stared at me.

Lacey's mouth was still open when another girl

piped in. "You actually bought a dress at Wal-Mart and are wearing it?"

I shrugged. "Yeah, it's cute."

Lacey rolled her eyes and whispered something in the other girl's ear. They giggled just as a group of the groomsmen rambled on about something stupid. Of course one of them was Beau.

If one were to Google stereotypical fraternity boy in the dictionary, more than likely they would find Beau's picture. He wasn't very tall, in fact, in flip flops we were the same height. He had the usual frosted tips and his hair was styled into a faux-hawk. He tanned regularly and didn't see a problem with it. He said it made his teeth look whiter.

He headed straight for me. I was almost knocked out by his cologne. It smelled like he had dumped the whole bottle on himself.

"Hey, Libby."

I didn't look up to see his dimpled grin. Instead I just focused on his tribal tattoo snaking around his bicep that poked out of the bottom of his pink polo shirt.

"Uh, hey Beau."

I tried to look for someone else to talk to, but it looked like the other bridesmaids were busy whispering and flirting with the groomsmen. Not that they cared that I was there anyways. I felt like I was in high school all over again. The outcast for being tall and blonde.

Mom used to always tell me it was because the other girls were jealous. I'm pretty sure they weren't jealous that I could spike a volleyball over their boyfriend's head in gym class.

"I guess we are walking down together. But don't get the wrong impression and all. I don't want your boyfriend to come at me with a pitchfork or something." He laughed obnoxiously, obviously thinking he was hilarious.

I rolled my eyes. I had a feeling that was supposed to be some kind of southern hillbilly joke. My arms were crossed over my chest and I tried to turn away as much as possible. I hoped he would get it through his head that my body language was telling him that I didn't want to talk. No such luck.

"Where is ol' Billy Bob or whatever anyways? I think I should be talking with the guy that's nailing my ex-girlfriend." He smiled that smug smile.

"He's not here." Lacey beamed. "So you can have her all to yourself." She pursed her lips together. Obviously something had gone down with Beau and Lacey, other than what I knew about. Unfortunately I just wasn't sure what.

"Alright, places everyone!"

A hefty gray-haired woman in a large pink muumuu clasped her hands together and pointed every which way. Sweat was already plastered on her forehead, but I think anyone would have that after dealing with a bridezilla.

Unfortunately, I was walking down the aisle with Beau. So he tried to give me his arm as we walked toward our space in line. I pretended like I didn't see it.

"So where is he, Libby?" Beau whispered while we waited our turn behind five other people.

The sweat was visibly dripping off of the muumuu-clad woman's forehead as she tried to point in every which way, guiding people to walk, as well as telling everyone else around her where things were supposed to go. I honestly felt sorry for her. Everyone else laughed at her expense, even the bridal party.

"I wonder if her, and Libby wear the same size Wal-Mart muumuu." I heard one of the other bridesmaids whisper.

Ouch, I know I had gained some weight over the summer, but really were these girls always this mean?

Then I remembered, yes, yes they were. It brought me back to my pledging days. Yes, they out ranked me, but was using the Sharpie really necessary? And having Lacey hand it to Beau of all people to use to trace my flaws.

I can remember asking questions about taking leadership roles. When I first started rush, I was told that I had the potential to be an executive board member. I remember even Kristi herself told me that I could be the next Kappa president. Then after I accepted my bid, and started the pledge process and it was like everything had changed. At first it was great, going to fraternity parties, and slumber parties in the common room. That was the fun stuff. But then that all changed.

Girls yelling during Chapter that everyone wasn't stepping up with their study hours. Having Nationals come and bust the house for alcohol. The house was supposed to be dry, but after they find twenty-four bottles of hard liquor and five cases of beer, it seemed like the house wasn't so dry.

And of course, it was the pledges and new members that took on the brunt of this grief. Even though the long established members were the ones living in the house who had brought the alcohol, we had to suffer. Our study hours were increased, we had to attend different seminars, everything that the older members should have been doing, but if they had most of the new pledge class go, then they wouldn't have to.

It was all of these things that for some reason, had just slipped my mind. Being the reserved person I just ignored it and let it shrug off my shoulders. But I didn't feel like being that Libby anymore.

I turned my head sharply toward Beau's direction and smirked.

"No, my boyfriend is not here at the moment, but if he was he would tell your STD-ridden ass to leave me alone." I nodded my head in Lacey's direction, not taking my eyes off of Beau. "And tell Lacey she should maybe double up on the herpes meds. I think you can see her sores from across Lake Michigan."

Beau looked down, not wanting to meet the fire in my eyes. The rest of the group kept quite as well. I heard someone mutter bitch, but that was the end of it.

This was not the same pushover Libby Gentry.

The rest of the night I was made an outcast by the bridal party. Beau couldn't even look at me as we walked down the aisle. Anytime I made a sound everyone turned the other way, and it usually was followed by more whispering.

I was just lucky that my sister agreed to be my date for the rehearsal dinner. I hoped I'd at least have someone to talk to. Then I forgot that my sister was a Kappa, so that idea was kind of thrown all out the window.

"Oh em gee, it's Beth! I didn't know you were coming!" Kristi shrieked from across the restaurant.

Every single person stared at us. Which is pretty easy to do in a traditional Italian restaurant since it's not very big and it was windowless and subdued with colors of crimson and black that surrounded us everywhere. We had a back room to ourselves that was lit completely by candles. The warm glow of the candles didn't do anything for an ambience, it actually just made Kristi's fake orange tan look even brighter. Like a glowing cheese ball.

Beth smiled politely as she usually did. That was the thing about us Gentry girls, we could usually fake a pretty good smile.

"I didn't think you would see us right away." Beth said as she kissed Kristi on the cheek. Funny that my petite, curvy sister would make a comment about not seeing her tall, chubby sister.

"Well I was looking for my little sister and my favorite alum, so of course I would spot you two right away!" She beamed. The fakeness was just dripping from her mouth.

That was the thing about Kristi, and all the other girls there. They could easily turn on the charm. If you were a basketball fan, for that five minutes they talked to you they would be the biggest basketball fans you'd ever met, even though they had never watched a single game. That's the thing about sorority girls, always in recruitment mode.

The rest of the girls joined us, acting like we were all the best of friends and I just hadn't made fun of Lacey's mouth sores. Which were completely visible, that or she just had some really bad collagen injections.

I felt like it was spring recruitment all over again. We had just gotten our pep talk about having alcohol in the house, and I had just found out that at least seventeen of the girls in the house had slept with Beau. But the president made sure that we all had our game faces on, so I had to sit there and smile as all these girls talked about how we were such great friends and had so much fun together. I wanted to pull my eyes out with a spoon right there in the middle of the common room.

After what seemed like forever I heard Kristi's mom's high, nasally voice, call us over to the big tables full of steak Sicilian, different pastas, and breads.

Kristi ran over to the waiting Gabe, who actually didn't look that thrilled to see her. Actually, Gabe never seemed thrilled to see anyone.

Gabe was some sort of Eastern European nationality and he always looked like he was pissed off. His big bushy eyebrows were always furrowed, and if he wasn't drinking or chewing something, he was usually trying to flex the little of biceps he had. I honestly didn't know what Kristi saw in him, aside from them both being on executive boards for prominent Greek organizations. Her family was rich, his family was made up of working class immigrants. She was a business analyst for a major insurance company and he was still looking for a job as an elementary school gym teacher. It was like night and day, but she seemed to love him.

But I guess people could say that about Blaine and me. We were the opposites on the outside. Everything about us seemed so different. Like we were star-crossed. But I still loved him. I didn't care if his family didn't own a condo in downtown Chicago, or that he had crazy bleached hair. And maybe Kristi didn't care about that with Gabe either.

Maybe he took her out for lunch every day and kissed her forehead, even though he wasn't that much taller than her. Or maybe that was just Blaine and me, and I couldn't help but miss him terribly. Seeing the way that Kristi looked at Gabe was a way that I never looked at Beau. But it was the same way that I know Blaine looked at me. I didn't have to change myself for him and do the baby voice. He liked me just as I was.

But I also had to face the facts that Blaine wasn't there, and I wasn't sure if he ever would be again.

CHAPTER 26

I couldn't sleep the whole night before. It was like that stupid yellow bridesmaid dress reflected off of every street lamp and every single car's headlights that passed.

The wedding wasn't until three o'clock, but we had to be at Kristi's parents by eleven to get ready. I dreaded every minute of it. Not only had I outcasted myself from my sorority sisters, but I felt like I was also on the outs with everyone back in Louisiana.

I tried texting Dina, but she hadn't heard anything. I started to think she, along with everyone else back in Elsbury, was getting annoyed with me. It was like I was stuck in the middle, not sure where I would fit. At one point I was at the top of the world and now I wasn't sure where I was.

Luckily, Mom didn't sleep much either. Slowly I opened the door to my bedroom to see light pouring out of the open door from her office. I crept down the hallway; the hardwood floor was so cold compared to the stifling hot floor at Aunt Dee's. I wondered how high my parents had the air conditioning up.

Mom sat at her desk, a huge stack of papers with pink highlighting marks all over them were strewn in front of her. She didn't even look up as she took a sip of her coffee and brushed back a stray strand of hair from her face.

I knocked on the door frame and cleared my throat to her get her attention.

"Oh Libby, I didn't see you there." She looked up at me then over at the digital clock next to her desk. It read six a.m. "You're up early. Excited for today?"

She took another sip of her coffee, peering at me with her chocolate brown eyes from behind black Gucci glasses. Did she really need more than one pair of designer glasses? Aunt Dee only had one pair, and I think they had been broken and battered more than once.

I shrugged and leaned against the door frame, crossing my arms across my chest.

Mom's lips tightened as she took off her glasses, absently running a hand through her hair and tousling it. "You know, I think things were a lot different when I was your age."

"Mom!" I sighed plopping down on the brown leather chaise that sat directly across from her desk.

"Don't Mom me, just hear me out." She took another sip of her coffee. "I'm a pretty good attorney, so I think I can make a pretty good argument." She shot me a wink and put her mug down.

I blew air out hard through my noise, not saying a word and just looked at her.

"You know when I was in college, if you were a girl, and you went to college, you joined a sorority. That's just how it was. And since my father was a frater he insisted that going Greek could only help my networking."

Mom's dad was also an attorney. She honestly didn't need to do any networking. After law school she joined his firm and eventually became partner.

"And you know it didn't hurt that I met your father during college either." She took another sip of her coffee, smiling at me.

"But, things were different, for me, for your sister. When you came home and told us you were going to be a Kappa, your father and I were thrilled. We thought you would finally come out of that shell you had buried yourself in during high school."

I rolled my eyes. "Mom, I wasn't that bad in high school."

"Libby." She stared me down. Those dark brown eyes were almost black.

"Okay, maybe I was a little reserved." I crossed my arms over my chest and peered out the window. The sun had just started to rise and was casting shades of orange, red, and yellow through the slightly drawn linen curtains.

"But, I soon realized that being in a sorority wasn't exactly the best place for you either."

I snapped my head back toward my mom. She was a loyal Kappa. In fact, her office actually still held pictures from her initiation and her pledge paddle hung proudly in our living room. I never thought I would hear her say anything even remotely unkind about a sorority.

"I felt like you lost yourself, Libby, even more. You just became this girl who I didn't even know anymore." She picked up her mug again, staring out the window.

"Then you went to Louisiana. And you know I wasn't for it as much as your father was." She glanced up at me quickly, before looking back down at her mug. "But he thought it was what was best for you, and I hate to say it, but he was right."

"How so?" I cocked an eyebrow, leaning in with my whole body.

Mom rolled her eyes as she stood up from her chair. "Libby. I know how much you didn't fit in during high school, and let's face it, I'm no stranger to the Kappa hazing rituals."

She took another sip of her coffee as she headed over toward the chaise, leaning in toward me.

"Libby." She patted my knee and sat down next to me on the chaise. "At one point I was like you too. Hell, I only joined Kappa because I thought it would be the only way to get ahead in college."

She slipped an arm around me as I bent my head into the crook of her arm, pulling my legs into my chest.

"And don't get me wrong, I met some wonderful people through Kappa. But I think by meeting your father and starting out in my first law firm, I really found out who I was and grew as a person."

She looked down at me smiling and brushed a stray curl from my face.

"And I think you are finally starting to take after your mother."

∞

I almost turned my car around on at least five different occasions as I headed toward Kristi's parents' house. After the wedding, she and Gabe would be moving into a small two bedroom apartment in Wrigleyville. But for now she lived at her parents' sprawling North Shore estate, which, I think, was twice the size of my parent's house.

I didn't really understand why her parents needed that big of a house for just three people. They were both doctors, so they were always gone, and Kristi was an only child. I wondered if they would be selling it after the wedding. Of course it would either have to be a huge family, or just a very wealthy one that would want to move into their house.

I took a deep breath and parked my car, just past the big gated entrance. All the other bridesmaids already had their cars lined up and down the driveway, and soon the limo would be making its circle around their giant Grecian fountain. We would all pose for pictures in our usual fake smiles with our hands on our hips right in front of the fountain.

I wondered what Blaine would say about all this. Would he change his opinion about me, knowing that I hung out with girls that lived in gated mansions? I almost turned back again and drove away, just thinking about it. I thought if I started right then I could maybe be in Elsbury by the next morning. Then I could give Blaine a good swift kick in the butt, and then go out to Café Du Monde with Britt until Blaine came and begged for my forgiveness. It sounded wonderful.

But Kristi was my big sister. She'd been there for me more than enough times. Every time Beau cheated, she was there; every time I just needed a shoulder to cry on, she was there. So instead of turning around I walked across the cobblestone path and headed through the front door into one of the longest days of my life.

∞

I think the makeup artist's job was to make us look like a bunch of beauty queen porn stars. I think that Kristi just said to her, you know, I just want them to look like a porn star decided to become the next Miss America.

The hairstylist's job was to put our hair in what I thought looked like modern bee-hives. The stylist straightened the hell out of my hair, paving through it with a flat iron, before piling it into a big over hair-sprayed pouf on the top of my head. I really looked like an X-rated, blonde Loretta Lynn.

I looked at myself in the mirror. I didn't even recognize myself past the inch of foundation and mile high false eyelashes. But it looked like Kristi was happy with her same painted face and mile-high hair. Well at least she seemed happy in between her snarling bridezilla moments. Her mom is a psychiatrist; she really should have slipped her something before she almost took down the florist and two bridesmaids. Now they were just casualties in the bridezilla aftermath.

Kristi had us all get in our dresses before the grand finale of helping her in her dress, which I think she needed all of us for. Her dress was an over twenty thousand dollar, custom-made gown that she had worked on with some famous designer in New York City. It was big, and over the top, and if you would have put a red wig on it and spray painted it orange it could have been Kristi's personality twin.

All the bridesmaids assembled in Kristi's bedroom.

Each one of us pulled our dresses off of the hanger, eager to just get them on. It wasn't the most flattering dress for every girl, with its low-cut sweetheart neckline and tea-length hem. But it was what Kristi wanted, and it was a very cute dress, at least on the hanger.

I slowly slid off my sweat suit and stepped into the dress. It was definitely a bit more snug since I had tried it on at the beginning of the summer. In fact, maybe a little too snug. In May, I had been able to zipper up the dress on my own, but this time it kept getting stuck at about the middle of my back. I called another bridesmaid over to help me, but she couldn't get it. So she called another girl over to help us.

"Oh it's not you honey," she cooed. "I think this zipper is just having some issues."

"Damn, how much weight did you put on Libby?" Lacey quacked from across the room.

She sauntered over toward us, a few other girls were snickering beside her. "You better not let Kristi see you. She will flip shit," she whispered before taking a big gulp of her champagne.

I wanted to cry. I knew I had put on weight over the summer, but I didn't think it was that bad. I didn't know what I would do. The wedding was in only a few hours, and my dress didn't fit. I was a big yellow whale.

"What's going on in here?"

I snapped my head to see Kristi in the doorway. Her hair was all done with her veil in it, but she wore nothing more than a white corset top and a pair of blue panties. I guess she was waiting for us to help her into her dress.

I froze when I saw her. I knew if she would have seen that my eyes were watering, she would have added that to the complaints that I didn't fit in the dress. Ruining the dress now the makeup, minus two points for Libby.

"Looks like your little, isn't so little anymore!" Lacey cackled along with a few other girls.

"Shut up, Lacey." Kristi snapped as she ran toward me. I never had heard her yell at Lacey before. Lacey was like her little pet. And I could tell Lacey was a surprised too, since her jaw was almost to the floor.

"Now what's going on?" She looked down and assessed the zipper situation.

"We can't get it to zip…" One of the girl's whispered, preparing for a meltdown.

"Kristi I'm so, so—" Kristi cut me off with a single wave of her hand.

"Don't worry about it, Libby." She turned toward one of the girl's who was helping me with my zipper. "Tiff, go get a needle and thread from my mom."

"Libby honey, you are gonna get sewn up in this bitch, so I hope you don't plan on getting lucky."

It was the first time I heard Kristi laugh all day, and I think it was the first time I had laughed in a while.

CHAPTER 27

With me sewn into my dress, it was time for Kristi to get into her giant ball gown. It took about five of us to actually get her into it, and then another three to smooth out the back and extend the cathedral train. I could see why she needed so many bridesmaids.

We all grabbed our flowers, pink Stargazer lilies of course, the Kappa flower, and headed into the giant stretch limo after a barrage of pictures in front of Kristi's house. I didn't know how much more fake smiles and posing I could take. I felt like it was recruitment all over again. But for the first time in this entire wedding process, Kristi actually seemed genuinely happy. She smiled and joked with the photographer, laughed at her dad's stupid jokes, and even gave Lacey some extra lipstick.

It was going to be a long day, and I knew that from the start. A day of watching two people profess their love to each other for all to see; when I had someone, whom I loved, who couldn't even profess his love just to me.

Now I was raised Catholic. My dad's family was from Louisiana, so naturally they were all big Catholics. My parents would take my sister and I to church every Sunday morning, followed by catechism afterwards. Once I was confirmed, we stopped going as regularly and became the Christmas and Easter Catholics. That was until I moved to Elsbury.

Like clockwork Aunt Dee would wake Britt and I up and we would go to church, followed by brunch with the bridge club. Instead of focusing on mass though, I usually focused on Blaine sitting in the pew next to me, and thinking how good he looked when he was all dressed up. But, Kristi and Gabe were neither Catholic, nor Southern, and Blaine definitely wasn't going to be sitting next to me looking very uncomfortable in a tie.

Kristi and Gabe's wedding was on the beach. Hundreds of chairs were piled up to the gazebo that met the shoreline as we pulled into the resort. How the staff managed to fit enough chairs for the four-hundred guests was amazing to me. The chairs were all lined with pink and yellow flowers with a giant white runner leading down to the gazebo where a nervous Gabe and the preacher stood.

The lady in the muumuu was, of course, there to greet us as soon as we go to the resort, clucking orders and lining us up with the groomsmen. I felt awkward standing next to Beau. Not just because he was my ex, but since Kristi had required that the bridesmaids wear three inch silver heels, I was way taller than him. I had to completely slouch, so that I didn't look like an Amazon woman with her captured prey.

Bach's Largo played as we slowly walked down toward the cascading waves of Lake Michigan, I couldn't help but scan the crowd for Blaine. The whole time during the ceremony, when I should have been paying attention to the vows and to Kristi, I kept hoping for one of those moments out of the movies. I thought that Blaine would just come in, interrupt the ceremony in some dramatic fashion, maybe running with a bunch of wait staff chasing him, and then he would profess his love to me. We would kiss in the middle of the aisle and then everyone would clap and some classic love song would play. Of course none of this ever happened.

The wedding ended, the bride and groom kissed, and people cheered as they walked out; UB40's *Can't Help Falling in Love*, played as we all walked back down the aisle.

Between the ceremony and reception we all assembled on the beach for pictures. Millions of the same poses, where we were supposed to look 'spontaneous' and 'natural,' but really we were just being directed by a very short Hispanic photographer with a lisp and bad goatee to 'smile this way' or 'act surprised.' I never thought one could be so exhausted from smiling. Of course, even though it was photography time, most of the groomsmen decided that the party had already started.

"Hey, hey Libby."

Beau's breath smelled like turpentine as he whispered in my ear. It was actually more of a quiet yell with his hot breath lapping against my cheek. We were stuck in some cheesy prom pose for about fifty frames and I was really getting tired of having his sweaty hands all over my waist.

"What, Beau?" I gritted through my teeth. I was still smiling, only because I had to for pictures, but my tone make it clear that I was annoyed.

"Isn't it awesome that there is going to be open bar

all night? It's like being VIP."

He staggered. The photographer had to stop at least six more times, just to make sure he got the right shot between a bunch of wobbly groomsmen.

"I really don't think you need to be having any more time at the bar, maybe you should head over to the hors d'oeuvres table."

He aimlessly waved a hand before going back into a shit eating grin and wrapping his arms around me. I wondered if he would be acting like this if Blaine was there, but obviously I didn't know what that was like. I was starting to think that I never would again.

The beach was transformed in what was only a matter of a few hours. Going from a beautiful, seaside wedding to a romantic reception. Dozens of tiki torches lined the beach, reflecting off the water and pairing with the fading sunset to create an array of oranges and reds dancing on the surface of the water. Table after table were decorated with lilies and candles, as men in tuxes carried trays of little canapés and shrimp.

I stood in awe looking at the twinkling lights above me, wondering how one could possibly string lights from mid-air like that. But my awe was quickly dismissed when Beau, and the other groomsmen, pushed their way past me to get to the bar. I swear I saw the bartender's eyes widen behind his bamboo hut when he saw ten guys in tuxes barreling toward him. I rolled my eyes again and headed toward the head table. I wasn't in the mood to drink, or to even be there. Being at the ceremony really made me realize, Blaine wasn't coming, and he probably never would again. I was really alone. But I would be okay.

I just wanted to get back to Louisiana more than anything. My mom was right, Kappa may have been the best thing at the time, but now it just wasn't me anymore, and I was really getting sick of Beau and his grabby hands.

∞

Dinner was as fabulous and over the top as the rest of the day. I never knew that seven-course meals actually existed, but apparently they did. Our faces were continually stuffed with dish after dish of food. Beau continued his flirting and didn't seem to get the hint that I wasn't interested.

"Hey, Libby. Hey, Libby," he slurred, leaning his whole body in to me. No matter what I did I couldn't lean away. He was practically spitting on my swordfish.

"What Beau?" I tried not to look at him, and create a barrier with my hand wresting on my cheek, while I swirled the asparagus around on my plate.

"You know I'm doing my internship at Trump tower in Chicago, so while you're living there I'll get to see you every day." He sounded like an excited little kid, albeit a slurring, stumbling one.

The night before, my sister had decided to tell everyone about her pregnancy, and somehow that led into the discussion about my parents moving. I almost completely forgot that Beau was supposed to be doing an internship there. It made me want to move back to Louisiana even more. Get the heck away from that train wreck.

"That's great, Beau." I didn't even look at him as I

spoke, staring blankly at my plate. Just because Blaine had left me didn't mean I was going to go crawling back to Chicago and back to Beau.

After the final course, Gabe and Kristi headed to the dance floor as the DJ announced it was time for their first dance. A slow country song played. I used to make fun of Kristi all through school about her love of country music. We were both wealthy girls from the Chicago suburbs, so her love of country music never made sense to me, until now. After being in Louisiana, and falling in love, I finally understood the meaning to all of those country songs. I could feel the tears trying to push through my eyes. Slowly I moved my chair back and tried to sneak away, but before I could, a cold hand gripped my wrist.

"Hey." Lacey slurred. "You can't leave yet, we have the bridal party dance!" She smiled a big toothy grin at me, like everything was just perfect between us.

I smiled weakly back and slid back into my seat, choking back my tears. Luckily other people were tearing up as well, so they just thought I was being sentimental. Little did they know what was actually going through my head.

Suddenly every song from the first dance to the father-daughter dance, made me think of Blaine. Thinking of all the times we would be riding in his truck and he would loudly sing along with some obscure song on the radio just to make me laugh, but I wasn't laughing now. I wasn't there surrounded by people I loved or who cared about me, except for maybe Kristi. Sometimes I didn't understand why things happened, but I guess everything does happen for a reason. I hoped someday I would see the bigger picture.

The DJ announced that it was time for the bridal party to join the bride and groom on the dance floor. The moment I was dreading. Beau couldn't hide his excitement. His clammy hand grabbed mine as we got up from the table. I was too emotionally exhausted to even resist. He pulled me close and I slid my arms around his neck, trying not to make eye contact.

"You know Libby, this is a sign," he stammered. "Why else would we be here dancing at Kristi's wedding if we weren't supposed to be together?"

I wanted to shout: because we were paired together as a bridesmaid and groomsmen for our friends' wedding you big oaf!

But I didn't. I said nothing. I just swayed in silence as the song played, and he continued to blabber on. Maybe this was where I was supposed to be. Maybe somebody was really telling me that this is where I belonged. Maybe I was always supposed to be the socialite with the boyfriend that cheats on me. I should have never gotten a taste of something else, because that wasn't where I was supposed to be.

But then I didn't know why it felt to right to be in Blaine's arms, sitting on a bench outside the antique shop. I didn't know why I felt more alive standing in Aunt Dee's kitchen and mixing a bowl of grits then I did while I stood with Beau on the dance floor. I was confused and just wanted to get away.

As soon as the song ended, I quickly slipped off the dance floor. Luckily, Beau had run to the bar as soon as the song was over and hadn't noticed that I left. My heels were sinking in the sand, so I quickly slid them off and started farther down the beach. The moon was completely full and reflected off the water, making it look like it was floating right on top of it. I walked as far as I could, while still being able to hear the wedding going on behind me, before sitting on a bench a few feet away from the water's edge. I dug my feet into the cold sand and it felt great against my poor feet that spent all day in very uncomfortable heels.

I pulled my phone out of my pocket. I looked at the picture on the background. I still didn't have the heart to change it. It was a picture of Blaine and me, when everything was still good. It was a picture I took on my phone the same night he had asked me to be his girlfriend. It wasn't exactly a flattering picture of either of us. He looked sunburned from spending all day outside, after one of the hottest days of the year, and I believe I had a milk mustache from an ice cream sundae. But no matter what I looked like on the outside, I could tell that I also looked genuinely happy.

It wasn't a fake smile like I had painted on in for all of the wedding pictures, but it was a genuine smile. A big toothy grin, I could have even been laughing. But I wondered if Blaine was really as happy as I was in that picture. I wondered if I was just a rebound, someone to keep his mind off of his ex-girlfriend. Maybe he was just a really good actor and I was just his latest role.

Looking down at that picture, I then realized, it wasn't just Blaine that made me that genuinely happy. It was everything about Elsbury. I never thought I would like it there, I always thought I would be the same sorority girl. The truth was that I had never felt more alive as I was when I was in Elsbury.

I wasn't labeled as just some blonde sorority girl, though I am sure some people thought of me that way, but once they got to know me I became something more to the town. More than I ever was before. I wasn't just a blonde sorority girl, I was someone's niece, someone's cousin, a girlfriend, a bookkeeper, I was more than I ever could have been had I stayed in Chicago.

The more I thought about Elsbury, the more the tears started to pour down my face. Big black blobs made streaks through my heavily powdered face before falling onto my lap. I was in full out sob mode and couldn't help it. I could faintly hear the sounds of the reception going on in the background, but I still felt more alone than ever as the sound of my own cries rang in my ears.

"There you are!" A voice cried as it approached me.

I recognized it as Kristi's and quickly wiped the tears from my face with the back of my hand and stood up. She looked like a stick figure that was stuck in a cupcake as she came toward me, holding the skirt of her dress up while she maneuvered through the sand in her giant heels.

"I have been looking everywhere for you!" She yelled.

"Don't worry about me Kristi. I'm fine, just had to get away for a bit." I tried to fiddle with my hair, but gave up, realizing it was a lost cause.

"Well I came to give you your bridesmaid gift," she exclaimed matter of factly.

"Kristi you already did that remember?" I pulled

the lavaliere out of my pocket. It had the letters KB dangling in white gold from a matching chain. We had to ceremoniously take the necklaces off after pictures since a Kappa was never supposed to drink with letters on.

"Not that." She waved her hand like she was swatting a fly. "This." She turned her shoulders and did a short, loud whistle.

Slowly from behind a large oak tree, a body started walking down the beach. I had to squint at first to see who it was, but as soon as he spoke I immediately knew who it was.

"Hey Libby." His voice was melodious and sorrowful all at the same time. I would know that accent anywhere. It was Blaine.

His blue eyes met mine as he approached, making a circle with Kristi and I. He was wearing the suit that we got him in New Orleans and looked just as uncomfortable in it as he did every time I would see him dressed up in church. I wanted to smile and at the same time wanted to hold back tears.

"How did you…when…?" I was flabergastered. I stumbled over my words as I tried to fight back the impending tears. It took everything I had not to embrace him. I wanted to smell his familiar scent and to kiss him again, but I couldn't tell what he was thinking and didn't know how he would react to me tackling him.

"Well on that note, I think I'm going to let the two of you have some alone time." Kristi patted my back. "I guess I should get back to my wedding, don't do anything I wouldn't do!" Kristi called over her shoulder as she headed back to the reception, cupcake dress and all.

I flopped down on the bench. My mind was racing so much that I was physically exhausted.

"So..." Blaine carefully sat down next to me, making sure that there was still a bit of space between us. "Some wedding, ey?"

"Why didn't you show up at the airport?"

It was all that I could say, and it just came out like word vomit. I couldn't even look at him, and I so longed to stare into his blue eyes and have him tell me that everything would be alright. Yet I couldn't. I just stared down at my bare feet.

He sighed and put his head in his hands. "I don't know."

"That's not an answer." I lifted my head up slowly, and turned toward him. "My dad always said that 'I don't know' is just a filler word when you don't want to say what you're really thinking."

I could hear the air blow out of his nose as he smiled. It wasn't a happy smile, more like one of frustration. "I missed your quick wit."

He didn't look up at me, but I couldn't help but just stare at him. He looked like a little boy that had just been punished for coloring on the sofa. It really made me want to reach out and touch him, to hold him in my arms, and just blurt out how much I missed him too.

"The truth is." He looked back toward the wedding reception and let out a deep sigh. "I can't compete with all of this." He waved his hand aimlessly in the air before looking back at the ground.

"I didn't ask you to." I was completely puzzled. I had no idea what he was talking about. How could he be comparing love to Kristi's wedding?

"I know the only reason Julie stayed with me was because I played baseball. It's no secret that she knew she was better than me."

He pulled at the sleeve of his suit while talked. It was obvious he was nervous, and wasn't used to spilling this much emotion at once.

"When I met you, I swore I wouldn't fall as hard as I did. I knew that we came from two completely different worlds. I looked up your hometown, one of the wealthiest suburbs was what it said, and I didn't know how a good old boy from the south was supposed to compete with that."

He folded his hands together and unfolded them again before he started speaking. I knew not to interrupt and to let him get it all out.

"Then you said that you loved me, and honestly I was completely shocked. That's why I didn't say anything the first time you said it. But Sunday, that was when it really hit me. I didn't want just some summer fling. To pour my heart out to you and then as soon as you went back to your hometown, you would forget all about me. Realize that I was nothing more than just some stupid southern boy that kept you occupied for the summer."

I thought about what Meg had said about Julie, and suddenly it was all clear to me. Blaine really did believe that I would leave him just like Julie did. He didn't come to the airport because he didn't love me. He didn't come because he did love me, and was scared to get hurt again. So instead of being hurt he tried to just let me go.

That was all it took for the tears to start coming in

full force, dribbling down my face.

"When you left..." Blaine finally faced toward me, wiping the tears from my eyes with his thumb.

"I felt like shit. I knew I had really messed up, so I basically decided to try and go into hiding until you came back, and then figure out what to do."

He looked down. For once he was afraid of my stare instead of the other way around.

"But then you called Jackson." He looked back up again, closing the gap between us as he moved toward me. "And you told me after all the hell I put you through, that you still loved me."

He smiled, putting his hand to my cheek. "And then I knew I really messed up."

I smiled weakly. I was still mixed with so many emotions I didn't know what to think.

"So, with no one else to turn to, I found Kristi on Facebook and messaged her. And let me tell you that girl lives on Facebook."

He smiled, letting the air blow through his nose as he did.

"She responded right away, and then she called me." He put his hands down and started playing with the sleeve on his shirt jacket. "She found that I could transfer my ticket over to today, but it might be kind of expensive, plus I would need to get a rental car."

He stopped fiddling with his sleeve and took a deep breath, exhaling slowly.

"Well, obviously I did it. But I didn't get to Chicago until about two hours ago, and then well, it's hard for a good ol' boy like me to navigate the city, so I did get lost a few times."

That I actually did laugh at. I could just imagine

Blaine in a little rental car trying to navigate the highway.

"I know I deserve to be laughed at. But the point of all this is that I'm sorry Libby, and I hope that you can find it in your heart to forgive me."

His eyes met mine; they had so much behind them. It was like we were thinking the same jumbled mess. Fear, hope, confusion, but most of all I knew that Blaine loved me, he may have not said it, but at that moment I knew he did.

I took his hands and intertwined my own in his. Slowly I leaned forward, closing my eyes to kiss him, when I heard a crash down the beach.

Blaine snapped back. We both opened our eyes and sprang up from the bench.

"What the hell was that?" He didn't let go of my hand as we turned to look behind us.

Scrambling to his feet with a now empty rocks glass in his hand, was Beau. He staggered toward us. His tux was covered in sand, and I thought there was even some sand in his faux-hawk. He smelled like he had been rolling in vodka and could barely hold up his own head as he came barreling toward us.

"What do you think you are doing with my girlfriend?" He slurred lazily and pointed a finger at Blaine.

"Your girlfriend?" Blaine glanced at me out of the corner of his eye. A smirk crossed his face and he let go of my hand, crossing his arms over his chest. "I don't know what you've been drinking there buddy, but Libby ain't your girlfriend anymore."

"What? What did you say to me?" Beau tried to stand up as straight as he could, but still was swaying.

"I said." Blaine stepped even closer as he leaned toward Beau, and made sure he enunciated every word. "Libby Gentry is not your girlfriend anymore."

"You dun know what you're talking about," Beau slurred and stumbled closer. Beau then mumbled something under his breath, but I couldn't understand it.

"What was that man?" A cocky smirk crossed Blaine's face.

"Blaine let him be. He's drunk." I charged past Blaine and tried to help Beau stand up straight.

"Get off me bitch, this doesn't concern you." Beau shoved me to the ground so quick I didn't know what hit me. Then he stood looking over me. My mouth was gaping open as his bloodshot eyes met mine. "This is between me and –"

But before Beau could finish his sentence Blaine's fist made direct contact with Beau's jaw. The look on Beau's face was almost indescribable. It was a mixture of shock and nausea as he fell flat to the ground.

Blaine turned away from Beau and grabbed my hands, pulling me up and closer to him. Slowly he slid his arms around my waist.

"Now, before we were interrupted." He pressed his forehead to mine while I wrapped my arms around his neck.

"I love you Libby Gentry. I have since the day I met you." He smiled. "And I guess I was too stupid to say it before."

"I love you too, Blaine Crabtree." I returned the smile, leaning in closer. "And you weren't stupid, Blaine." I nodded my head down in the direction of

Beau. "I was the stupid one. I shouldn't have tried to force you into anything."

"Trust me Libby, you didn't force me into anything. It was a long time coming." He pulled me closer as he spoke, tightly wrapping his arms around my waist.

"You know I would have never thought that a guy like me would land a girl like you. When we first met I just thought you were some sorority princess, but then I got to know the real you. The girl that has more insecurities than anyone, but deep down is the girl that will go out of her way to make everybody happy. The girl who doesn't hold anything back, and the girl that had my heart from the first time that she yelled at me."

And then he kissed me. With the world going on around us, Beau whining like a scared puppy in the sand, and the music of the reception playing in the background, but nothing else mattered. It seemed like it was just the two of us, standing on the beach, in love.

CHAPTER 28

"As soon as we get back to Elsbury, we are getting you a bigger car." Blaine protested as he adjusted his seat for the millionth time.

"I think you secretly like my car and you are just too embarrassed to admit that your girlfriend has a better car than you." I glanced at him out the corner of my eye.

It was almost three a.m. by the time we finally left the reception. Well, not all of it was spent at the reception...some of it did involve the beach...and my car...and the beach again... I was so happy that Blaine came to the wedding, but I still couldn't get out of my head what my mom had told me earlier that day.

It was before I left for Kristi's house. She walked into my room with an envelope secured with the University seal. I almost completely forgot that I had sent in to appeal to get back into school.

"Well, aren't you going to open it?" My mom pressed.

Wasn't that my goal of the summer? To eventually get back into my parents' good graces and to go back to school? It seemed so simple at the beginning of the summer, but while I stared at that letter every emotion ran through my head. I would be sad to leave Aunt Dee in Louisiana, but maybe I would be happier once I was back with my friends. I mean, I would be closer to my sister and my new niece or nephew. Chicago was a lot closer to school than Louisiana. I was also still very confused about my romantic relationship at that point. I had filled out the appeal form and requested letters of recommendation after one of Blaine and I's many arguments. So, with a long drawn out breath, I ripped open the letter.

When I read the first word as 'Congratulations,' I knew the appeal was successful.

"Earth to Libby." Blaine waved a hand in front of my face. "I've never seen you concentrate so hard."

"Oh yeah, I was just thinking."

We pulled into my parents' driveway and Blaine looked like a little kid who had just seen his first candy store.

"This is your parents' house?"

I put the car in park and turned off the ignition. "Yup, well at least until they move into the new condo."

"Wow I don't know how you are ever going to be able to leave a palace like this for Aunt Dee's little place in Elsbury."

I wondered if I would have to. It wasn't like there was anything that was really keeping me in Elsbury. I loved Blaine, but I was sure if we really did love each other he would understand my need to finish school. If I stayed there with Blaine would I end up just some small town girl? Going to the diner every night, and be barefoot and pregnant before I turned twenty-one? But then the other side ran through my head. What would happen if I did go back to school? Could I even pass another year at school, or would I just fail out again?

Blaine reached across the seat and grabbed my hand, leading my eyes toward his.

"You are coming back to Elsbury, right?"

I bit my bottom lip and tried not to meet his gaze.

"Well..."

He set a brochure on the dashboard in front of me. "This was kind of my trump card, if you didn't want to go back after I poured my heart out to you." He leaned back into the seat. "I honestly didn't think I would have to use it."

I picked up the brochure, looking at the seal on the front and a picture of cattails. St. Joseph community college was scrawled in an old English text on the front. I'd never heard of the place. In all reality the only school I knew of near there was Tulane, and that was only because Don went there.

"Blaine, what is this?"

"I've known all summer that you were itching to go back to school. I knew there was no way that you would stay in Elsbury just for me, no matter how hard I tried."

He took my hand into his and started tracing lines in my palm with his fingers. "So I picked one of these up, talked to an advisor, and they said your GPA didn't matter you could start from scratch.

I stared down at the brochure. Speechless. I didn't know when he did all of that and couldn't help but be in awe on how amazing he was for doing it.

"I also know that you applied for appeal to get back into Illinois State."

I shot my head back toward him.

"Libby, you're not very secretive about anything you do, and after Googling what happens when someone gets kicked out, I knew your lawyer mom would have you file for an appeal."

"That doesn't mean that I can just go to some community college. What about the antique shop? What about work? This is still forty-five minutes from Elsbury and I don't even know if I'd have a car to get there."

Everything was like a big, giant mess. All these little pieces of paper were compiling one big blanket that was taking over all of my thoughts. Did I stay in Chicago and go back to school, so that I could stay closer to my sister? Or did I go back to Louisiana and take a chance with a new romance?

"So, what do you want Libby?"

No one had ever asked me that. It seemed like no one had actually ever cared what I wanted. At that moment when I had the choice of what I wanted to do, I had to be absolutely sure that I was making the right one.

"Well you do know how important school is to me, so I should probably think what would be the best for my future," I said, slowly, still staring at the brochure.

"Does this mean I am going to have to plan a lot more trips up to Illinois?" Blaine asked.

I slowly shook my head, looking up to meet the blue eyes that I fell in love with. "It means you better get used to having a St. Joseph community college student as you girlfriend."

ABOUT THE AUTHOR

Magan is a self-proclaimed geek-to-glam poster child who channels her inner geek by writing science fiction for teens. Even though she slept with a nightlight until middle school for fear of alien attacks. She now lives with her husband, daughter, and dog in central Illinois where she still sleeps with a nightlight…just incase.

You can find her online at www.MaganVernon.com.

OTHER WORKS BY MAGAN VERNON

My Alien Romance Series:

How to Date an Alien

How to Break up with an Alien

How to Marry an Alien

Anthologies:

In His Eyes Anthology

Made in the USA
Charleston, SC
25 March 2014